ARDENT HEART

ROMAN SEMCESEN

Published in Australia by Sid Harta Publishers Pty Ltd,
ABN: 46 119 415 842
23 Stirling Crescent, Glen Waverley, Victoria 3150 Australia
Telephone: +61 3 9560 9920, Facsimile: +61 3 9545 1742
E-mail: author@sidharta.com.au

First published in Australia 2018
This edition published July 2018
Copyright © Roman Semcesen 2018

Cover design, typesetting: WorkingType (www.workingtype.com.au)
The right of Roman Semcesen to be identified as the Author of the Work has been
asserted in accordance with the Copyright, Designs and Patents Act 1988.

Semcesen , Roman
Ardent Heart
ISBN: 978-1-925230-37-6
pp240

About the Author

Roman Semcesen migrated to Australia from Eastern Europe in the mid 60's. He is a family man who is married with two children and two granddaughters.

He is a professional signwriter by trade with hobbies of artist painting and writing both fiction and children's stories.

His first published book *Ardent Heart* is an accomplishment which was achieved by the help and support of his family.

CHAPTER 1

The quaint coastal town of Plymouth in England was well known for its fishing exports to other countries. It was a calm and clean place in which 1920 society could live, work, and play. The majority of townsfolk who lived there were regarded as being dirt poor, while the minority were considered to be quite well off and rich in wealth.

Inland from the coast, the town became surrounded by mountainous landscapes as far as the eye can see. There could also be found, the Plym River, a fast-flowing water course that ran through the heart of town, dividing the place into two main districts. The rich lived on one side, while the poor took up residence on the other.

The mouth of the river stemmed from the mountain peaks nearby, gushing through the town and descending further down, into a big waterfall and rock pool below.

The rich district and poorer slums were connected by a rickety old wooden bridge, in great need of some heavy maintenance. The cost involved to repair it was a hot topic of local dispute and discussion, among rich and poor alike.

The rich townsfolk boasted they never needed to use the

bridge. Because of this, they felt that spending money to repair something they never used was an awful waste of resources. The poorer community expressed great concern about the cost of repairs and maintenance: this was something they could not afford to pay. This left them no choice but to leave it as was, which was unusable. Constant disagreements about this matter meant the bridge was left untouched.

In the wet season, with large rainfalls, the river would swell and break its bank, where major flooding of the bridge would ensue. For the poor, it was a nightmare to think about the bridge collapsing. The rich were not worried, as they had the river ferry situated close by.

The ferry carried not only people but also coaches, horses, stock and other cargo. The community called it *The Henderson's Ferry*.

❡

The Henderson family had acquired the ferry several generations back. Roger was a young man when it first came into his possession. Being such a dedicated person, he decided to live and work on the ferry full-time. He used to say it was so much better for his customers too, which helped him to serve them properly.

Roger was a most honest and trustworthy person. People could always rely upon him, impressed by his moral and work ethics. He adopted the attitude that "as long as everyone's happy, this was the most important thing" and in turn, this made him happy too.

❡

Working onboard the ferry was not an easy job to carry out. He used to start early in the morning and would finish late at night, seven days a week, come rain, hail, or shine. After he took control of the ferry, his wife, Regina, became angry about what he had chosen to do, all for so-called 'tradition', but felt powerless to change the situation.

Eventually though, the husband and wife separated. Regina went to live in her own house in the same town of Plymouth, while he stubbornly stayed on the ferry.

Roger and Regina had two adult children, Peter and Elena. They were much loved by both parents. Roger referred to Elena as 'my dolly'. This began when she was young and continued to this day, much to the annoyance of Elena. Still, she chose not to make an issue of it out of respect for her elderly father. She paid him regular visits on the ferry, and on each occasion, he greeted her by pinching her cheek.

❡

The small cabin possessed huge cracks in the walls, through which the wild winds could blow, while the roof of the ferry was covered in metal sheets. In wintertime, it was extremely cold and miserable, but in the summer months, it was like living in a sauna. On wet days, the rain insisted upon falling where he ate and slept. Buckets were scattered everywhere in the living quarters aboard the ferry.

The bed he used was made of unyielding wooden planks with straw thrown on top, to give him some padding. Roger covered this with a dirty sheet, his pillow stiff and greasy. It was rare he would wash anything– linen, clothes or dirty dishes. He was known to be a heavy smoker, having the occasional drink. In his busy times (which were quite often), he ate on an irregular basis. Sometimes, he would eat some proper food but only once a day.

Roger often wished he could live a better life, but could not abandon the Henderson family tradition. So begrudgingly, Roger stayed as he was, alone and without his family who did not understand.

After a long day's work, all he could think about was getting a good night's rest.

⁋

Because of the unhealthy and difficult lifestyle he had chosen to live, it finally had a negative major impact on his body. He started showing signs of weakness and realised he was not as strong and resilient as he used to be. His hands were becoming wrinkled and stiff with arthritis, while his legs were grew weaker with age. Roger suffered constant pain each time he walked, but being bred tough, he smiled through it all. Except occasionally, he would lose his composure.

'Oh, dear Lord, my life is getting worse by the minute,' he would complain to certain passengers.

'Mister Henderson, you're overworked, tired and run off

your feet. You need to retire gracefully,' they kindly suggested, but their caring words fell on deaf ears.

'It wouldn't be fair to leave you lot to swim to the other side while I lay resting. My dear passengers, my purpose is to serve you with all my heart, for as long as it continues to beat,' he would say.

Because of the long hours he kept, his health worsened rapidly, his coughing more and more laboured, making it difficult for him to breathe. Roger knew he was seriously ill, but for him to admit that to anyone, except to himself, was simply not on. He remained persistent, continuing the good fight and stand up for the Henderson clan, whatever the cost.

A head full of false pride, sometimes while talking to someone who cared enough to listen, Roger would slam his fist down hard against the cracked and rotten timber table.

'I am what I am. Nobody can change me, nobody! I'm a Henderson through and through, until the day I die. End of story.' And wanting to make sure he got his point across to his listeners, he would then sometimes yell and kick the table leg in frustration, which caused him to cry out in great agony and pain.

His daughter, Elena, was getting very worried about her father's welfare and bravely approached him with some common sense. She hoped he would listen this time.

'Dear father, what about leaving this type of work to someone younger and seek a different type of job that's less stressful and which has shorter hours. At your age, it must be playing havoc on your health. What do you reckon?'

Roger was not too impressed with her suggestion, but asked

out of curiosity, 'my dear sweet dolly, what do you mean when you say for me to seek a different type of job?'

'Father, you can always come back to town and spend the rest of your life in an easier one that requires a lot less physical demand, and which will give you more free time to relax with your family,' she stated.

He blew out a large puff of pipe smoke before commenting. 'My beautiful dolly, it's easy for you to say that, but you don't realise the family value and honour of being part of the Henderson clan. It's all about the history that creates this unbreakable wheel of tradition turning, even today. And now, you wish for me to end it, for no real worthy excuse. Oh no, definitely not. I cannot and will not do it.'

Elena looked at him with great concern, as tears rolled down the sides of her sad face. She realised then he was inflexible and stubborn to the core. No wonder her parents agreed to separate.

'Please, dolly, go home. Grow up into a beautiful woman, tease some nice boys your own age. Then, at the right time, you can get married and have children of your own, who can all be perfect little miniatures of you,' her dad helpfully mentioned.

Fully realising her father was ignoring her request, Elena reluctantly turned to leave. She forced a false smile upon her face, in order to make her father feel happy. He affectionately pinched her cheek and in return. She leant in close to kiss his unshaven cheek.

❡

Some three years passed and before she was aware of it, Elena did grow into a beautiful young woman. She has long blonde curly hair, perfect blue eyes, possessed a nice enough figure and was of average height.

With the money she saved, Elena bought a ladies' hat shop in town. She was exceptionally skillful in her job as a salesperson, with an open and honest nature. She was always on her best behaviour and thought carefully before she spoke to her customers.

Like clockwork, Elena would be there on time each day, to warmly welcome everyone who walked through the door of Glory Hats. Whether they were young, old, rich or poor, she treated them all as being equal. She had been the owner of this shop for quite a while now and selling her wares came easy, because she believed in the quality of the products she displayed.

At one stage though, she had been pondering the idea of trying something different, in another location nearby. Elena seriously discussed this possibility with her mother, whose opinion she greatly respected.

'Mother dearest, because I've been working so long at the same place now, I'd like to try my hand at doing something that I haven't tried before. What do you think?'

Regina was somewhat taken aback by her daughter's suggestion. 'Oh, dear child, I personally think this job is just right for you. You're smart and your customers know what to expect. You provide a great service, you truly listen to their needs and you're friendly. Besides which, they all love you. I believe they would be totally lost if you were no longer there helping them,' she replied with all sincerity.

Elena listened with gratitude to her mum's advice and decided to continue, for the time being at least.

¶

Meanwhile, Regina started thinking about her daughter's future in regard to marriage and children. At one stage, she attempted to gently initiate a conversation about this same subject with her. 'Elena my dear, you are now an adult and are independently living separately from home. You are your own boss, so to speak. I therefore think it's about time you consider the possibility of finding a lifelong partner you can marry and have children with.'

'Oh mother, you are so old fashioned.' Elena laughed, hugging her firmly.

'That may be so, my dear, but I still want to be a grandmother.'

'Mother, I think my boyfriend has not been born yet or is still sucking on his dummy. So, we will both need to wait a while,' she jokingly answered. With this flippant yet firm response, their conversation ended.

¶

On each subsequent visit to her father, Elena found him growing frailer by the day. He looked so pale, was unable to move very well and was having great difficulty with his breathing and speech. She was devastated to see this once strong man in such bad shape. She was most concerned.

'Hullo, Father, how are you feeling today?' she asked, with trembling voice, about to burst into tears.

'Fine, I feel fine,' he hoarsely replied, with a hacking loud cough.

'I love you so much and beg you to start thinking about leaving this place at once. Please, please, I implore you to look after yourself,' Elena urged.

'My daughter,' he raised his voice. 'A job is a job is a job, and a Henderson never gives up, regardless of the circumstances. It's important to be of service to others, rather than simply thinking about yourself all of the time.'

'But Father, this work is always going to be here for others to carry on, but your health may not be. I consider our health is more important than anything else in the world. If you don't have that, then you have absolutely nothing,' she replied, disagreeing with her father's belief.

'Ah, my little dolly, you can't change the cards that life happens to deal you with. One day, everybody will leave their job and physical life too. It's far better to live, where you can feel a strong sense of belonging. This is my ferry, this is my tradition, and this is me,' Roger said, coughing and gasping for air.

'Oh, my dear father, please try and look after yourself better. I wish you well,' she said quietly and firmly; inwardly struggling to hold back a flood of tears. She hugged her dad warmly and assured that she will visit him again soon.

After a few days passed, still feeling restless with anguish about her father, Elena paid him another visit, as promised. She was horrified to see his situation had got far worse, so quickly. As he was now coughing up blood!

'Oh, dear Lord,' she whispered, trying not to panic. 'Please Dad, I think you badly need a doctor, immediately.'

'A doctor, what doctor? There's no doctor that exists on Earth who can help me, dear daughter. They are quite worthless creatures really. Nope! I'm still alive, for better or for worse and this is all that matters,' he responded, aggressively. He then softened his tone somewhat and added, 'my dear dolly, you just look after yourself and quit worrying about my health. It really is quite unhealthy for you to do so.'

'Okay, but I'll come and see you again real soon,' she said, hugged him and left in a hurry to see her brother, Peter, to talk about their dad's long-term welfare plan.

§

'Oh Peter, what I can say, it's really bad,' she spoke, with fear.

'Elena please, tell me exactly what's happened?' Peter asked, in dazed surprise.

'Oh, dear Lord, I've just returned from our father, only to find he is more than sick. He's now coughing up blood and even I know this is not good,' she informed him, bursting into great sobs of sadness.

'Oh no, I can't believe it,' he shouted in anger. He quickly grabbed his hat, rushing towards the open front door. 'Elena, I'm going to see and talk to him myself,' he said. Without wasting any more precious moments, he went directly to the ferry.

¶

Roger saw Peter approach from a distance and shuffled the rest of the way to welcome him aboard the ferry.

'Hello, son. You just missed your sister. She was here only half an hour ago.'

With no preamble, Peter got straight to the point. 'Father, please tell me, how are you really feeling?' He was in shock to see how his dad was in such poor health. 'I see you're working non-stop as per usual, which is affecting you in a bad way. We all know your job is important, but your health and overall wellbeing should always be your first priority.'

'You're beginning to sound like Elena. We've had this discussion as well, many times before and now you. Oh yes, my son, I know full well that's what you all think but what each one of you keep forgetting is, that I've chosen to represent the Henderson family. Where the job comes first, and health comes second,' he said, while coughing and would not back down from his tough stance.

'But father ...'

Roger interrupted Peter with his gravelly voice. 'No, don't. Enough is enough. My son, if I'm going to die, it'll be right here on the ferry,' he stubbornly confirmed.

¶

Feeling greatly disappointed with his father, Peter returned home to still find Elena waiting for him. They discussed the situation, which both concerned them greatly. Together, they decided to appoint a medic from the town to examine their father's physical condition and frantically rushed to Dr Flannery's office, explaining to him the facts, as well as requesting he should see their father.

'Well, why not, that's what I'm here for. Please send him to me immediately,' the doctor proclaimed.

'Oh no, you don't understand. This would be extremely difficult for us to arrange. You see, our father is extremely old fashioned and pig-headed. He doesn't like change, which includes being away from his ferry for too long. We know him very well, Dr Flannery, so can you please save him?' they both pleaded. 'Personally, we feel that time is quickly running out for him, as he is now coughing up blood.'

The doctor digested this last bit of information with great gravity and shook his head in dismay. 'Well, Mister and Miss Henderson, my duty is to help cure all sick people who come to me, but those who literally cannot come, the doctor is obliged to visit them. So please tell me, can your father still walk?' he enquired.

'Yes, he does but his movements are very restricted and slow,' Peter said. 'Please, we strongly suggest you visit him, before it's too late.'

In such a situation, Doctor James Flannery agreed to pay Mister Henderson a visit on the ferry. He hurriedly seized his medical kit and headed off.

Roger was surprised to see a man with an official looking black case boarding his ferry.

'Hey, who goes there? Are you an inspector of some sort or are you a tax collector?' he asked the stranger, with interest.

'I'm neither one of those, but I am Doctor Flannery. But let's not be so formal and feel free to call me James,' he said.

'Well, would you like me to take you across the river then, James?' Roger asked.

'No, Mister Henderson, but I am here to examine the state of your health,' Doctor Flannery peacefully uttered.

'What, you wish to examine me! Why?' Roger asked, after which he coughed and spat on the ground.

'I want to help you, sir.'

'Who, me? What business is it of yours? Are you serious? I don't believe you. Who sent you?' he angrily enquired, spitting on the ground again. James saw the blood present in his spit that time, but chose not to react to the fact that Roger was indeed very sick.

'Mister Henderson, your two adult children came to my office earlier today, begging me to come and help. I can now see for myself you are seriously not well.'

'Ah, now I understand. It was my children who put you up to this. I told them not to worry.'

'They are. And quite frankly, so am I. So please, will you allow me to do my job?' the doctor demanded, while taking another step closer to Roger, but was quickly stopped.

'You mean you haven't finished what you've come here to do? In fact, I think you'd be far better off as a mechanic repairing my ferry, rather than running around finding new patients for yourself.'

'Mister Henderson please, I just want to do my job. So please let me do at least that much,' James pleaded.

'All right, fine. If it'll make my children happy and will get them off my case, then let's do it and let's get it done quickly,' Roger responded, despondently.

The doctor shook his head in frustration, opened his kit on a dirty table nearby and pulled out something which resembled a gauge with a pump that you could squeeze.

'What's this thing? It looks like some kind of a hand pump for a wheel. It's too bad that my ferry doesn't have any wheels, otherwise I would have bought it from you,' Roger laughingly said, in a mocking and sarcastic tone.

Ignoring Mister Henderson's remark, James went on to explain. 'This here is an instrument for measuring blood pressure.'

'Get away from me. You're not going to suck out my perfectly good Henderson blood with your evil-looking siphon,' Roger warned, as he spat out a large amount of bright red blood into his well-used and crumpled handkerchief.

'Mister Henderson, can you please take off your shirt?' Doctor Flannery politely requested, pulling out a new instrument.

'Are you mad or what? Why do you want me to remove my shirt?' Roger furiously queried.

'Okay fine, you don't have to, but can you at least undo the top few buttons, so I may place my stethoscope upon your chest, to listen to your heartbeat.'

'Hey, take it easy there, mechanic. Even without your weird looking gadgets, I already know what I have within me. I know

I have a heart and lots of tough guts. My heart's strong and reliable, like a ticking clock and my guts are full of … well, guts,' Roger laughingly exclaimed, but did relent by unbuttoning his shirt.

The doctor gently touched his hairy chest with his stethoscope, listened for a moment and then shook his head in dread.

'Is it all in tip-top shape, doc, or is it sick, like the brain in your shaky head?'

'Be patient please. Once I finish, I'll happily give you my prognosis.' He tried to laugh, but choked from lack of clean air and strong fumes.

'Dear mechanic, my prognosis is that tomorrow is going to be a fine day,' Roger grumbled.

The doctor nodded his head and continued. 'Just a few more general tests and I'll be done.' From his little black bag, he proceeded to bring out and grip a small rubber hammer, which he used to knock Mister Henderson's knee with.

Without warning, Roger jumped up from his seat and quickly brought back with him a huge steel hammer, which he now casually held in his hands.

'You see here, this is the Henderson's hammer that's over two hundred years old! If she makes contact with something, she really hits like an earthquake. Would you like me to test it out on your own knee?' he asked with glee.

'Oh no, no, most definitely not!' the shocked doctor shouted, promptly putting the rubber hammer to one side. He thought it would be wise to simply tap Roger's knee with one finger instead.

'Now Mister Henderson, can you please open your mouth wide for me,' he asked gently.

'Open my mouth! What the hell for?'

'It's simply a part of the overall examination, which lets me know if you're healthy or not.'

'Well, if that's the case, I must be real healthy, because I still have all my own teeth. Feel free to take a good look around,' and opened wide for the mechanic, who was posing as a doctor.

While peering inside and whilst holding a small torch, James could clearly see a quantity of pooled blood and again shook his head. 'All right, thanks Mister Henderson. You can close your mouth now.'

'You see, I'm all right. They are real Henderson teeth and they don't belong to a rat or a skunk either. So, do you believe me now when I say that I'm fine?'

The doctor merely nodded, while not replying to his question on purpose.

'And before we go any further with this examination, it's now my turn to see your teeth,' Roger seriously demanded.

'What, you want to see my teeth?' James asked, surprised at this strange request but reluctantly agreed to open his mouth to show Mister Henderson his own set. He did acknowledge that he did have one tooth missing, but all the rest were relatively well maintained.

Seeing this, Roger was both impressed and sardonic. Impressed to see the level of care the doctor took with his teeth and sardonic to see that one was missing, which caused him to laugh hysterically in a comical way. 'You see, I'm much older than you but your teeth look much older than mine and one is missing, where I have all mine. So, what do you say now, Mister Toothless Mechanic,' he scorned. 'I tell you, Henderson's teeth are the best in the world.'

Upon hearing this, Doctor Flannery felt greatly ashamed and chose to move the conversation on quickly to a different matter.

'May I examine your ears now please?' he enquired, his forehead was now profusely sweating due to acute embarrassment about his missing tooth.

'No, no can do. My hearing is perfect, as it was for my father and Grandfather Henderson. You don't need to repair my ear. So therefore, you don't need to look into it. Sorry,' Roger declared.

¶

After this arduous and long examination, James succeeded in carrying out most of the tests and observed that Roger was suffering from a bad chest infection, pneumonia, bronchitis and the common cold.

'Mister Henderson, your health is in a serious state of decline,' the doctor finally emphasised to him. 'But if you listen to my advice, there is a chance you will become better again.'

Roger attentively listened before finally responding. 'Hmm, you said become better and after that better, will still come the bad! And pray tell, who, when, where and how can you cure the last bad? Now please, take your junkie, rusty, and broken-down tools and leave me alone. Nobody in this world can stop death, not even you. Goodbye, mechanic, and have an interesting life.'

With persistence, James said, 'Mister Henderson, I'll come and check on you at some other time.'

'I thought I just said goodbye to you,' Roger said as he glanced at his big hammer sitting next to him.

This caused Doctor Flannery to leave Mister Henderson in quite a hurry, knowing this man's true intentions. He reflected that he had many patients in his life, but none quite as bad as this old, tough and uninformed man. The doctor shook his head and returned to town, feeling powerless to assist.

Peter and Elena were waiting patiently for the doctor to return from his visit. Upon entering his office, James sadly informed them both about their father's health situation, as well as his personal conclusion that Mister Henderson is indeed a most stubborn and very sick man. Of course, Peter and Elena had already known these facts, but in a strange kind of way, felt better for having it confirmed by a professional.

9

Roger slowly lost his strength and became weaker by the day. Because of this, he requested his son should visit him, which he did without hesitation.

'My dear Peter,' Roger said with a sense of resignation in his voice. 'Please listen to me. I'm a sick old man and my life is getting shorter and shorter. I feel that I'm not going to live for too much longer!' Roger then fell into a body-shaking, bone-rattling, coughing fit. 'My son, for the sake of the entire Henderson family generations that have come and gone before me, I beg you to please take over the ferry when I'm gone and serve the people as I have done all these years. They need your help. You must keep the family tradition continuing for years to come! Please son, please say yes. I need to hear you say it.'

'Yes, Father, I will do as you ask,' Peter said, his heart breaking. He thought about his dad's terminal condition and hugged him firmly. 'I will do my best for you!'

In his turbulent mind, from this point onwards, he began to think about how he would need to readjust his lifestyle.

Chapter 2

Peter Henderson lived the life of a peasant. He was used to working in the fields, ploughing, sowing, harvesting, and attending to other agricultural activities. He owned horses and poultry, as well as a variety of other domestic animals. His charming wife, Anna, worked with him. But mostly, she spent her time at home looking after their little son, Adrian. making sure he always went to school five days a week.

They were considered to be a successful couple, who lived a worthwhile life. People respected them for being honest, reliable and friendly.

Since that day when Peter's father asked him to run the ferry, his entire life changed. Peter became indecisive, about what to do and how to implement certain changes which needed to happen. Initially, he spent numerous sleepless nights loaded with inspiring plans, heavy questions, and uncertain answers. *What now? Which way do I turn to start living again, where I can keep everyone happy?* Peter kept going over these questions, asking himself repeatedly what to do. but found it difficult to find a viable solution.

At the same time, Plymouth's locals had their own dilemmas and asked themselves, *what will happen when one day our old ferry man, Roger, will leave us? Who will take over the ferry? Will the new owner be honest, friendly, good-hearted and punctual as Roger was?*

¶

One cold morning, just before sunrise, the people gathered on the bank of the river, waiting to go across to their respective jobs and begin their work day. They spoke about a broad variety of topics, such as health, jobs, the economy, family and the ever-increasing prices of groceries, sports, clothes, and more. They rubbed their hands together, trying to keep themselves warm. While talking with each other, they were continuously glancing over at the stationary ferry, at the other side of the river. Time quickly passed, growing later and later. People were beginning to get impatient and nervous, while checking their watches every few minutes.

One person from the crowd suddenly asked what everyone else was thinking. 'Why is the ferry still not here?' And so began to panic; the ferry did not have any lights on and there was no smoke coming from the chimney either.

'Oh, my Lord, it's about time to move the damn ferry. What's happened?' other impatient passengers asked themselves and each other.

'Maybe the ferry man is still sleeping? How long will we have to wait, or he might have a young, pretty woman keeping him company and he's forgotten all about us?'

'You must be joking. Have some sense. man. He's too old and not physically capable for that sort of thing! Hmm, this doesn't feel right at all. I've noticed in the recent past where Roger has become overtired and did not look at all healthy, poor old man.'

'To hell with that! All I care about is that I'll be late for work. My boss is of the shifty and unforgiving nature- he could sack me on the spot, no questions asked!' said another person, complaining.

'Damn the stupid, old fool. He should have told us before-hand if he wasn't going to run the ferry today. Shows he's not a decent and honest man,' another one piped up, stoking dissatisfaction's fire.

A responsible and caring person then stepped forward, trying to pacify the angry, waiting passengers. 'Please, please, ladies and gentlemen. As far as I know, Roger Henderson has always been most honourable, punctual, reliable and respectful to all. We should face the possible fact he may be extremely sick … or forgive me for saying this Lord, but he may even be dead. Who knows?'

'Well, if that's the case, who will come and move us across the river then?' another person yelled. not having any compassion for a moment about Roger's welfare.

❡

In the wee small hours of that fateful morning, while the town still lay sleeping, the gravely ill Roger took his own life, quietly hanging himself. On the bedside table, he scribbled a suicide note with the words, *'I feel better now, because I've decided to die on my own terms. I chose to end my life before the Angel of Death could come and pay me a visit himself!'*

The news of Roger's death did not come as a surprise to the local people. They had known for a while he had been extremely unwell and may leave them any day soon. However, they were shocked to discover the way in which he passed away, greatly puzzled as to why he killed himself.

§

When word about Roger's death finally reached his family, Peter and Elena were in disbelief. Peter accepted the suicide a bit more easily than Elena, who was totally devastated to know he took his own life. Peter called the doctor to be with her. He gave Elena a dose of sedatives to help her get through this most difficult and emotional time of her life.

For a few days, the ferry was out of operation and all regular commuters needed to use the bridge as an alternative means to cross the river.

§

Peter felt as though he had no choice but to fulfill the promise he made to his father. This was the only way for him to move on and start a new life. And so, he began working on the ferry, a transformation from a life working on the fields to working on the river. He planned to relocate his family to live on the ferry as well, but later realised this was virtually impossible. The operations room was far too small for an entire family to live in and his son, Adrian, certainly could not be expected to travel daily from ferry to school, as the distance was far too great. The only solution for Peter was to continue living with his family while travelling to the ferry for work every day.

§

In the beginning, Peter found the work to be an arduous chore, with the new time schedules and unfamiliar work environment, including the overall job description. Not to mention the people, as they too were the basis of much worry and bafflement for him. After a while though, Peter quickly came to be respected and understood by the commuters, giving his passengers little reason to complain.

'He's only a beginner, but he'll come around. He's a Henderson after all,' was the general vibe travelling throughout the community who used his services.

§

His job and personal commitment required him to wake early each morning. As a farmer, he'd never bought a car before, as he never previously needed one. Now he felt the strain of not having one. Each day, his primary mode of transportation from home to ferry and back again would be either walking or riding his bicycle.

He worked diligently throughout the day and almost always returned late at night. His wife, Anna, understood and accepted the unbridled naive passion he devoted to his job, in loving memory of his dad. In turn, he comprehended her struggle of raising Adrian in a house where father and son rarely ever met. For both, it was a difficult time; a true test of their marital resilience. This new kind of lifestyle went on for a few weeks before anything would change.

§

With each passing day that Peter spent at the ferry, the family environment grew increasingly tense. One day, he and his wife talked about finding a solution to make both their lives a lot simpler and easier.

'My darling Anna, guess what? I've devised a plan which will greatly improve our living arrangements,' Peter exclaimed.

'Oh Peter, what's your plan? Please tell me. I'm all ears,' she replied with a growing sense of curiosity.

'Well, what if we move to a house in a different location, much closer to the ferry. This would make our lives so much easier to manage and would put less stress on all of us,' he suggested.

'Oh, Peter, that sounds like a great idea but how can we possibly afford to do that?' she enquired.

'Sweetie, my plan is that we rent this house to a tenant, while you and Adrian can go and live with your mother. She has a substantially-sized home located closer to where I work, than where we are now. I'm more than sure she'll agree,' he remarked.

'Oh yes, I so love your brilliant idea, Peter,' she said, shouting with joy.

'You see, the way I figure it, if you go and live at your mother's place, I'll have more time to attend to the ferry. You will have fewer worries about the house, more time for yourself, as well as looking after Adrian and your mother. For myself, because of the nature of my work, I'll split half my time residing on the ferry and for the remainder of the week, I'll live with the family I adore and want to be with so much,' he emphasised.

'That's great, Peter. Let's begin putting your plan into action then,' Anna happily recommended.

¶

Anna's mother, Katherine, has been for many years a widow. She lives on the outskirts of the village in a big timber structure which has five massive bedrooms and is surrounded by a luscious green garden with a smattering of colourful flowers. Katherine is a most likeable and animated woman, who manages to keep her home sparkly clean and well organised.

A few days after their discussion about her husband's proposed plan, Anna and Peter travelled to her home, to speak about what they had already decided. Much time was spent in creating small talk, before discussing the more important purpose of their visit.

Anna began the conversation. 'Mother dearest, both Peter and I are in the process of changing our lifestyle.'

'Are you now, how so?' Katherine questioned.

Peter briefly recounted to her details of the earlier talk he'd had with his wife.

'Can Adrian and Anna come live with you temporarily please, till we get our financial and accommodation difficulties sorted?' Peter asked.

'Of course, they can,' she remarked, without hesitation. 'You can move in whenever you wish. I have heaps of room and lots of spare space here, so you tell me when and it will be done,' Katherine added agreeably.

'Thank you so much. You see, I propose to live a double-life,' Peter responded awkwardly.

'A double-life? What on earth do you mean?' she asked, feeling somewhat bewildered.

'I'll be living some of the time at your place and a little bit on the ferry, in order to make my work life as ferry man easier. I also realise I don't want to make the same mistake as my father did, by living continuously aboard the ferry. I don't think that's a healthy thing to do, as I have family responsibilities as well,' he firmly stated.

¶

The idea progressed as discussed. Peter's wife and son moved into Katherine's abode, with Peter occasionally living there as well, while their original property was rented to another middle-aged couple named Martin and Vivien Prescot.

The new tenants of the house were peasants like Peter and Anna. They spent most of their time working in the fields just to sustain themselves. However, this family worked extremely hard and was relatively well known in the area. Quite often, they were hired to do tasks for people in a superior position, who lived on the other side of the river. They were always highly praised and recommended to anyone in need of physical labour.

If the people say this family stays true to their word and are reliable, then I will trust them as well, Peter thought.

Things in general kept getting better and better for Peter and Anna. Of course, there were some inevitable ups and downs, but the couple had not felt this happy or at ease in a long time. His family got used to Peter spending a few days on the ferry and then a few days with them, which continued as a cycle over and over again.

Life goes on, Peter believed. He was mighty glad he didn't have to live full time in his workplace, as his father did. He worried too that if he had done so, he might have even become like his old man, conservative, rigid, and restrained.

Peter recalled what his father once said. 'This is my ferry, boy. I've lived here my whole life and will continue to do so, and no one can stop me. Not even you.'

Peter however adopted a broader, more advanced view towards family, work, religion, and life in general.

'Ah, the church, why do I have to go there myself?' his father used to say. 'Let the God-fearing parishioners pray for my soul. I am the Lord's child too, so what's wrong with that?'

For Peter however, church was not just a place of prayer. It was a safe haven where you could socialise, listen, and learn from each other. His philosophy was that life always offered something new and interesting, which kept everyone spiritually connected to each other.

On the ferry, he slowly readjusted to his new way of life. For better time management, he hired a casual to give him a hand. When he took his one day off, usually on a Sunday, he would call in the assistant to take over the duties.

¶

One tranquil Sunday morning during breakfast, as they all sat around the kitchen table, Peter turned to Anna. He mentioned, 'today I have a day off from work and because it's so nice outside, I thought it would be a good idea for us to head to the church for a bit? What do you think, my dear?'

'Oh Peter, you took the words right out of my mouth,' she replied, with surprise. 'Of course, my darling, it would be wonderful to speak with some people I wouldn't normally get to see.'

'Okay well, that's settled then. After church mass, I request we go somewhere for a picnic. Perhaps the local park would be the perfect place or in a field of wild flowers, the lake or even near the river,' Peter uttered.

'Oh yes please, let's do it,' she responded, and arose to kiss his prickly unshaven cheek.

'Can I come too?' Adrian glumly asked, thinking he would be left out of the fun.

'Of course you can, son.' Peter then turned and grabbed his shoulders. 'We are doing this all for you and we will enjoy this special family time together.'

'Yahoo!' Adrian shrieked gleefully. 'Dad, I always like it when we go outside. There's always something new to see, to touch and explore.' Adrian got so excited, he began singing a song he had composed with the help of his music teacher.

'Now go quick, and get yourself ready. We have no time to waste,' he instructed, and they all left to change their clothes.

After a while, Peter emerged clean-shaven, with combed hair, was dressed in formal attire and had applied some cologne.

Anna, who was also attractively dressed, came out into the main room, standing bold in front of Peter.

'Oh, my dear, you look very handsome. I love you so much,' she enthusiastically said, kissing him with passion. 'Now please tell me, how do I look?' she asked, primping and preening in front of him.

Anna wore a pink and green silk dress with long sleeves and matching pink hat. Her brown hair was straight, which was always neatly combed and held together with a large pin.

'You look absolutely gorgeous- every inch, the perfect rose. No man on Earth has such a beautiful wife as I do,' he praised, bowed slightly and gave her another warm kiss on the lips.

The combination of bright colors on her outfit, blended with the rich vibrancy of her face and shades of gold from various jewellery, were the basis of her beauty. Seeing these features work together so well, Peter again complimented his adoring wife. 'It's truly amazing! Sometimes I can't even believe such an alluring woman like you could ever be married to a simple man like me,' he remarked.

This made Anna feel as if she were extra special. She took great satisfaction in receiving such openly warm and pleasant compliments.

Peter tried to be an affectionate husband. He fully understood Anna's personality and employed said knowledge to his advantage, when needed.

Anna was a healthy woman who is in the prime of her life. Since moving into her mother's place, she'd had more time to look after herself and be more presentable in public, but her inherent nature was secretive, she always liked to be the centre of attention.

The townsfolk would often compliment them, saying: '*she has a marvellous husband. He's so clever, dedicated and understanding, which gives her no reason to be ashamed of him.*' On other occasions, you could also hear them commenting that, '*he is one lucky man to be married to such a beautiful and charming wife. She's friendly and always a pleasure to be with, is good looking and is equally intelligent as he.*' While others would casually mention, '*Anna is such a quiet woman. She doesn't talk a lot, but is highly sensitive in an emotional kind of way.*'

¶

All three boarded a coach and went to St Benedict's Catholic

Church, while Anna's mum, Katherine, stayed at home. Outside, people were milling around, talking and waiting. On the rooftop, the bell started to ring, indicating morning prayers were about to commence. People entered when hearing the constant peal of the resonating bell. Some church-goers were already inside, kneeling and praying for their souls, asking for forgiveness and recompense for their sinful actions from the great Lord.

Father Greene presided over the church service, carrying the Bible. He approached a few visitors to engage in friendly conversation. However, in his haste, he suddenly realised he had forgotten something important in his room and later returned.

g

The organ played quietly in the background, a strong whiff of sage and frankincense flowed through the open doors and windows, irritating the noses of some sensitive people, who were forced to wait outside until the stench subsided. On the other hand, there were another group who were greatly attracted by the scent and preferred instead to wait inside.

The people who chose to wait outside were happily conversing amongst themselves, when suddenly a bird flew overhead relatively close to the ground.

'Oh, look at that beautiful bird,' a fine gentleman said, as he looked at the clear blue sky. As soon as he made this complimentary remark, the bird shat on his shoe.

'Oh no,' he bellowed. 'Oh well, I should count myself lucky. It missed my head.'

The crowd around him exploded into great gales of laughter. When the hilarity died down, a single voice suggested they should move under cover for better protection.

Amongst this group stood Elena, who was there mainly to listen to the church sermon, sing hymns, and pray for the soul of her deceased father.

After church mass was over, Peter left his family for a moment to meet with Martin Prescot.

'It's so good to meet you again, here of all places. Pray tell me, how is the condition of our property. Is it to your liking?'

Martin replied, 'Mister Henderson, everything is fine.'

'I'm so happy to hear that, sir. You can stay at my property for as long as you wish,' Peter acknowledged.

'Oh, thanks very much. We are most grateful. And Mister Henderson, we wish for you to swing by any time you want to as well,' Martin invited.

'We'll definitely keep this in mind, but not today. Some other day perhaps, sometime soon,' Peter promised.

They continued conversing for a little while, before they concluded their pleasantries and parted ways.

§

Peter and his family proceeded with carrying out their plan to have a picnic. They travelled by coach, far away from home to a place near the river, surrounded by emerald green forests and grassy ground. They found a quiet spot to relax, under some shady trees, to protect themselves from the full force of the sun. And on this particular day, no one else was present. They had the entire place to themselves, in which to eat, walk, drink, rest, talk, and play.

'Ah!' Peter sighed with relief. 'This is a perfect field in which to relax. Just look around you, my dear Anna. Mother Nature is indeed most generous with her gifts.'

'Yes, Peter, there could not be a better place than this. It's here that people can truly unwind and dream. As well as wishing never needing to return to their humdrum real world. I'm so glad we came here today, and thank you for suggesting it in the first place,' she confirmed.

¶

The waterfall was the best tourist attraction in the region. All year round, massive amounts of water fell freely from a great height, making a loud thundering noise that echoed throughout the place and beyond. As if nature whispered to those ears that would but listen: 'come swim, listen, touch, and feel my presence. Once done, you will never wish to leave me.'

Right on top was a massive rock, used as a lookout point to glance over the edge and into the river bed. On into the wide valleys, colorful fields, luscious forest and endless chains of mountains.

A long time ago, Peter came to this same spot as a child. Nothing much has changed, except for the fact that Peter was now a committed family man with a gorgeous wife and inquisitive son. However, this trip was the first time for Anna.

'Oh Peter, this is where I want to live for the rest of my life. What do you think? Would you care to join me?' she asked in awe.

He knowingly smiled and winked as way of reply.

As they rested and enjoyed the sunshine, a light wind blew into the woodlands, encompassing them with clouds of mist created by the crashing water from the waterfall.

This same mist brought with it a refreshing vibrancy and warmth. In the midst of all the euphoria, the three of them had a common thought on how nice it is to be here, to simply enjoy.

Adrian started to frolic merrily in the fields, extending his arms and pretending to fly. Amongst other things, the young boy tried to catch butterflies and then pretended to be drunk by falling on the ground.

Peter was near the horses, caressing their well-maintained manes. 'Hello there, my four-legged friends. I can tell you too are greatly enjoying this place as well.'

At this time, Anna collected wild flowers found in the field, manipulating them into a floral wreath, which she proudly placed upon her head. She approached her husband and happily asked, 'Tell me, Peter, how do I look?'

'Oh, you are my beautiful flower, Anna,' he honestly replied, smiling from ear to ear.

'I think I'll take this wreath home, to remind me of the wonderful day we've had together,' she joyously announced.

¶

After a subdued and lengthy time, the afternoon sun began to fade into the horizon and the environment altered its colour palette. An incoming cool breeze and the change in hue from yellow to bright red indicated a conversion from afternoon into evening.

'Well, dear family, I think it's time for us to go back home,' Peter declared.

'Home, oh no, not home,' Adrian demanded. 'Oh Dad, please don't say that. Look around and see how beautiful it is here. How can you possibly say we have to go? Couldn't we stay a touch longer? It's not dark yet,' he begged, with a gloomy face. 'Besides, if I were you, I'd stay here permanently.'

Peter looked at his son and wondered about how enticing it must be to have a mind of a young child. In answer to Adrian's previous comment, Peter then spoke. 'I tell you what, we'll come here again next time, I promise.'

Adrian, all at once, felt calm again as he heard his father utter these words.

'Dad, guess what?' he suddenly declared.

'What?' Peter asked, anxiously.

'One day, I'll come here by myself. Can I do that?' Adrian proudly asked.

'Oh yes, why not, my son? Of course you can,' Peter automatically replied without thinking any more about it. He then swiftly turned on his heels to prepare the horses for the arduous journey home.

'As everything in life has a beginning and an end, so does this beautiful day, as well. With our Lord's help, we'll arrive back safe,' Peter said with emphasis. They then all boarded the coach and slowly headed off.

'I'll see you again real soon, perfect place,' Adrian muttered under his breath whilst waving goodbye.

Peter and Anna took no notice of what Adrian just said. As they were both lost in their own separate thoughts about the great and natural wonder that they had just witnessed.

§

The nickname of the place they just visited was Mystery Waterfall. The people of Plymouth and other villages nearby called it that. Why it was called this, was also a bit of a mystery.

Many strange stories circulated around the waterfall, and some of these stories changed a bit over the years with every retelling. But the strangest ones of all stayed the same.

There was a story about a man who went swimming in the river directly beneath the waterfall, but no one saw him come out, so he was presumed dead. When they later went to look for his body, it could not be found. It was concluded he must have drowned and floated down the river, with the help of some strong and swirling currents. A few days later and by some miracle, he boldly walked back into town, wearing completely dry clothes and was very much alive and well.

Some people even claimed to have seen a man stupidly jump from this same site late at night, who found himself unexplainably stuck halfway down. The same people also said that after this event, an orange light glowed brightly for a few seconds every midnight, in this exact spot. Others even heard weird and inexplicable sounds in the same vicinity. There is no particular or distinct pattern as to when this sound can be heard.

On another occasion. a young man walked into the police station and declared he had jumped into the near bottomless depth of the river as a sixty-eight-year-old and swam out as a twenty-year-old man. His wife, who was sixty-six when this event took place, one hundred percent backed up her husband's story. She swore it was the truth.

Many determined people have tried to explain this strange phenomenon, but no one has yet found any logical explanation as to how or why.

CHAPTER 3

Peter was curious to know how his rented property was going, so he travelled over to his old house. The day was still and humid. Once on the farm, he found Martin in the middle of a sunflower plantation.

'With Lord's help, how is the new tenant?' Peter said, reaching in for a friendly handshake.

'Ah, hello there, Mister Henderson, I thought you were someone else for a second. I see you have accepted my earlier invitation. It's so nice to see you again. It's always a pleasure to have proprietors, such as your good self, come around and see how things are going,' Martin said, greeting Peter in a jolly tone.

'You flatter me too much,' Peter said, trying to keep a new level of enjoyment out of his voice. 'Personally, I believe the real owner is the one who ploughs the land, plants the crops, harvests them and bakes the bread.'

'Oh, Mister Henderson, you're too kind,' Martin said as he lowered his head in humility.

Standing in blazing temperatures in the middle of this field of gold, both men wiped their sweaty brows: a result from being directly hit with the intense heat from the sun. Both wore straw hats in a futile attempt to circumvent these uncomfortable effects. Just then, a thirsty bird landed on Peter's straw hat, looking for some water, but soon realised it would be better to find what it was looking for elsewhere and so flew away.

Peter bent over and picked a sunflower from the vast myriad that surrounded him. He keenly observed the flower, smelling its perfume.

'Oh dear, I can tell there'll be an excellent harvest this season,' Peter happily mentioned.

'As they say- good year, good manure: good work result and good owner. All leads to a good harvest,' Martin remarked. 'And on top of that, Mister Henderson, I have great people like you, visiting me too.'

Peter simply smiled and said nothing. Jointly, they decided to go into the cool of the house, so they could escape the fiery furnace outside.

'Today is so hellishly hot!' Peter emphatically stated, trying to get his point across.

'Well, let's have some cold drinks then,' Martin suggested and called out in a loud voice, 'dear wife, where are you? We have a visitor. It's Mister Henderson.'

'I'm here, you don't have to shout,' his wife complained, as she breathlessly came running from somewhere else inside the house.

'Peter, I'd like to introduce you to my wife, Vivien. Please bring something cold for us to drink, dear,' Martin instructed and then turned to face Peter. 'Please sit and make yourself at home.'

The two happily sat and discussed the topic of agriculture, as they waited for their refreshments to arrive. Suddenly, Martin slapped himself on the forehead in dismay. 'I'm so terribly sorry. I forgot to ask about your wife and son. How are they?'

'They are both fine, thank you,' Peter honestly replied.

'Mister Henderson, I'm a bit curious about the ferry and your job. Do people still use it on a regular basis?' he enquired.

'Ah yes, it's still operational. You see, a ferry is smaller than the bridge and will never sink. The bridge, on the other hand, could be swept away with gusty gale force winds and raging waters,' Peter explained.

It was then that Vivien emerged with some cold drinks, placed delicately on a tray. 'Oh, Mister Henderson, it's so nice to see you. Please have something to drink, so you may cool down from this terribly hot weather we're having,' she politely said. Once securely placed on the table, she continued. 'I'm sorry I can't join you but will be back a little later to check on you both.' She quietly left the two men to continue their conversation.

'You know, Mister Henderson, Sam is coming home soon,' he informed him.

'Oh, and who is Sam?' Peter asked.

'Sam is my son,' Martin proudly replied. 'He is studying agronomics. He's about to finish his degree and become a professor of the subject.'

'Oh well, congratulations then are in order,' Peter enthused.

'When he comes here, we'll have an opportunity to talk

to him in depth about agricultural issues in general,' Martin explained.

'And how long will he be staying with you?' Peter enquired.

'Well, we expect him to be here for at least five weeks.'

'That is positive news indeed. One day, my wife and I will return and meet him while he's here.'

'This would be perfect, Mister Henderson. As I said, you're welcome any time,' Martin replied.

'Thank you,' Peter said, most happy to hear about Martin's son coming home. They continued to chat for some time before Peter was ready to leave.

'Oh well, the day's passing by, while Anna and my ferry are waiting for me, so I shall see you again soon, Mister Prescot,' he said, as he climbed on board the coach, whipped the horses and left.

Vivien then made her reappearance. 'What, has he gone already?' she questioned her husband.

'Yes, my dear Vivien. You've just missed him. You're too late to say, so long. Perhaps you can catch him next time,' he replied, as both went inside the house.

Martin must be a lucky man to have such a brilliant son. It's going to be interesting to meet him, Peter thought.

⁊

'Ah, you're back. What's the state of our property, pray tell?' Anna enquired.

'My dear, they are really extraordinary people who are

diligent in their work ethics and they're keeping our land in good order. This year, they're expecting a bountiful harvest as well,' Peter proudly remarked. 'And before I forget, there's one more thing; the new tenants have a son. He's a student of agronomics and is coming to visit his family soon. I think he'll stay for a few weeks. It will be nice to have a discussion with an expert like him. One day, we'll visit in order to become more closely acquainted.'

¶

After a week had passed, Peter, Anna and young Adrian were preparing to pay a surprise visit to the Prescot family. It was drizzling outside. Peter went to his room and got dressed in his everyday attire. When Anna saw what her husband was wearing, she objected immediately.

'Peter, please! You are a ferry man. Everyone in town knows and respects you, so please go and put on some clothes more befitting of your station in life.'

He grumbled something under his breath, but decided his wife was indeed correct. He put on a three-piece dark blue suit, which Anna had picked out for him. After putting them on, Peter looked like an entirely different man and sought out his wife's approval.

'Oh my, you look so handsome and dashing,' Anna said happily and kissed him.

She always dresses so perfectly for any situation, Peter contemplated. On this occasion, she wore a long brown skirt and a white silk blouse with long sleeves. She accessorised her outfit with a small pink hat upon her head and unashamedly added a large amount of jewellery and rings. In particular, Anna loved wearing gold, as often as she could.

'My darling, why don't you ever buy a different hat from the one which you normally wear?' Peter asked.

'Ah, ah! Let's not start that again. It's my head, my hat,' she firmly replied, silencing him immediately.

Anna finished her preparations by taking her pink handbag, to match her hat. Adrian also got dolled up and looked quite dapper.

With them all ready to go, they went outside to the waiting coach. Because it was still drizzling consistently, this fact made the road muddy and quite boggy in places. Which meant it was extremely difficult for the poor horses to pull the weight of the coach and its precious human cargo. Peter, from time to time, whipped the horses in order to make them go faster.

It was twilight when they arrived at their old house. The family pet welcomed them on their arrival. Martin heard the dog bark and peeked through the window, put his raincoat on and went outside to see Mister Henderson with his family and welcomed them with surprise.

Before he had a chance to say anything, Peter quickly said, 'hello Martin, we're here as promised. Although it's now pouring with rain and is hellishly windy, we still came because we thought it's now or never.'

With humility and respect, Martin invited the guests inside.

'Oh, Martin, we are soaked and wet to the core,' Anna not so subtly added.

'Don't worry, fair lady. A warm welcome and some warm words will help warm you up in no time at all,' Martin joked. Anna was not exactly amused by his response.

They went into the corridor, hung their coats on the hangers and left their umbrellas outside to drip dry on the veranda. Meanwhile, Martin's wife entered the room, wiping her hands on a crisp and white linen apron. She greeted the Henderson family and went immediately to the kitchen to bring some drinks. Martin requested the Henderson's to sit down in the parlour where they could be comfortable. A roaring log fire had been previously lit, as they congregated around a small coffee table and Vivien re-emerged with biscuits and tea.

'Any news, Martin, since my last visit here?' asked Peter, curious to know if Sam had already arrived.

'News? What kind of news do you mean?' Martin responded, later realising what Peter had meant. 'Oh yes, yes, of course.' He pointed to the side door with emphasis, where Sam stood near the doorstep.

He was of athletic build, tall, charming, with a droopy Mexican moustache. He was nicely outfitted and wore a pleasant smile.

'This is my son, Sam,' Martin said with enormous pride, as he introduced him to their guests. Sam walked further into the room and bowed to everyone present.

'Hello, I'm Sam,' he said and shook hands first with Peter.

'Hi there, Sam, and this is my wife,' Peter replied, forgetting to mention her name.

Sam extended his hand to her, in a gesture of welcome.

'I'm so pleased to meet you,' he said, while his seductive hazel green eyes subtly crisscrossed her body and held her hand a bit longer than usual.

'My name is Anna. I'm Anna Henderson,' she exclaimed with a slightly trembling voice, still gazing at his roving eyes.

I've never touched such soft hands in all my life. They are so warm and gentle. In contrast, my husband's hands are rough, like the bark of an old and gnarled tree. While continuing to reflect, she casually observed Sam in her feminine way and quite literally, could not get him out of her mind.

Sam thanked them for coming to visit, in spite of the bad weather.

'Thank you, Sam,' Peter and Anna said together.

Peter glanced over at his flushed wife and observed she was still hungrily staring at Sam. Anna then suddenly shook her head and came back out of her own deep and mindful meanderings.

'Yes, but we are wet, dirty and I feel quite uncomfortable,' she mentioned.

'Good quality rain is important, as it is like gold for all agricultural produce- no water, no life,' Sam replied while emphasising its importance.

Anna kept thinking, *so he's an agronomist. This would explain a lot of things, as he is obviously a well-educated person who understands the life of crops, soil and water. This would surely equate to him understanding people in general as well- their feelings, points of view, their suffering, satisfaction and love. Oh, dear me, I really must stop these random thoughts,* and sighed.

'And you! What's your name, young man?' Sam asked, as he diverted his attention towards their temporarily shy and withdrawn son.

'I'm Adrian.'

'And where do you go to school?' Sam asked with interest.

'I go to the local Plymouth State. They must like me, because my teachers compliment me quite often,' Adrian replied, now more forthcoming and enthusiastic.

'Ah, you must be an grade-A student then,' Sam praised. 'Believe in yourself and one day you'll become someone important,' he added.

'Tell me, Sam, when you were young, were you good at school?' Adrian openly began to ask a question, but he was interrupted by Anna.

'Adrian, please do correct your behavior, please call Sam 'Mister',' she warned him, as Anna started to feel embarrassed.

'Alright then, Mister Sam, how did you perform at school when you used to go there?' asked Adrian.

'Oh well, to be honest with you, I'm still there,' he awkwardly confessed.

'That's weird. How come you're an adult, but you're still at school. You must've done something really bad.' Once again, his mother quickly stepped in and interrupted for a second time.

'Adrian please, why are you talking in such a manner? Listen, Mister Sam is an agronomist, which makes him very smart,' Anna angrily said.

'Ronrom! This is so funny,' Adrian scratched his head

and went to Peter. 'Hey Dad, Mum said that Mister Sam is a ronrom. Tell me what this means exactly please?' Adrian continued to enquire.

'My son, don't be afraid to ask Sam what an agronomist is. So, go, he won't bite,' Peter advised.

Adrian walked back towards Sam and asked what a ronrom was.

Sam briefly explained what an agronomist was and what he did. After his explanation, he did not hesitate to give Adrian a big hug, while winking at Anna. Who coyly blushed, a strange and tingling feeling coursing through her body.

Peter and Martin continued talking about property matters. Adrian, feeling a bit bored, left his mom and Mister Sam to their own devices, while he flicked through some books he had found earlier in the house.

'And Mrs Henderson, where do you live?' Sam quietly asked Anna.

She briefly told him and was most happy to be asked that question. He is indeed a true gentleman. It's pleasant to know he's interested in me and my young son.

While Martin entered another room to fetch something, Peter took the opportunity to casually walk over to his wife and Sam.

'I'm so sorry I went to talk with your father and leave you both alone for a bit,' Peter said apologetically to Sam. 'So, please tell me, how's your study progressing?'

'Well, Mister Henderson, I'll be finishing soon and getting my degree in agronomy and after that, I'm planning to come back to live with my parents,' Sam respectively replied. He then glanced at Anna, who had not taken her eyes off him for even a split second and continued the conversation he was having with Peter. 'I heard from my father you work as a ferry man. Is that correct?'

'Yes, indeed it is,' he confirmed. 'You may know that Plymouth's ferry has been in the Henderson's family for quite a fair number of generations now. I'm continuing the tradition and hopefully one day, my son may do the same but only if he wants to.'

'Is it a difficult job? What with the inclement weather, people and other things, it must be awfully unsettling to handle on a constant daily basis. That kind of intense job must not be for everybody?' Sam enquired.

'Well it is for me. I do it for the people and the continuation of the Henderson tradition,' he proudly said and thought he was strangely beginning to sound like his pig-headed father. 'One day, Sam, I'm going to show you my ferry, if that's alright with you?' he concluded.

'Oh yes, that would be most interesting, thank you. But I should tell you that I've never been on a ferry before. We'll have to pick a nice sunny day to make sure the ferry stays afloat,' he joked.

'Aha, I get you, but why? This is very unusual, taking into consideration with what you are doing, but it looks as if the rain can scare you sometimes too,' Peter mentioned with a laugh.

ꞡ

The rain outside was now pouring down strongly, while lightning strikes lit up the night sky as if it were day, and the rumbling thunder was loud enough to make it seem like the landscape was shaking!

'You see what you've done, Sam. You brought us lots of rain and that's a mighty fine thing. And if the weather gods choose for it to continue raining heavily, we may have to stay the night,' Peter decided.

'Why worry about such unimportant issues? If you want to make sure you get home next time you travel in the rain, just bring your ferry with you. It may come in handy,' Sam said in jest.

'Hmm, I'm not entirely sure this would be possible. Oh well, let it rain then. If it should flood, then it is our Lord's wish,' Peter quipped.

'In a real heavy catastrophic flood, we'd have to start a new life, as Noah did with his ark,' Sam pointed out as he winked at Anna, who gently closed her eyes and sighed.

9

After a while, it did stop raining. 'Mom and dad, I want to go home,' a bored Adrian reminded them.

'Not quite yet, son, we'll stay a bit longer and then we can go,' Anna whispered to him.

'You can talk to him, but I'm not interested in your adult chats,' Adrian answered, quiet but determined.

Sam, whilst peering through the window, did not hear

what had just been said. 'Did you observe how the rain started and stopped all of a sudden? What an amazing natural phenomenon. Just like our lives, it begins and finishes suddenly. Nobody knows when it will happen and there's not a man alive who can change it. It is not within our power to do so,' Sam stated to no one in particular, still looking thoughtfully out to the fields that lay beyond.

Anna intently listened to him though, trying to absorb his every word. She wondered if Sam was always such a charming and well-presented young man or was he simply pretending? Anna enjoyed his sense of humour, his style, his unique way of thinking, and his philosophy, including his kind and gentle behavior. They were all a good source of pleasure for her; especially when his eyes were looking in her direction.

Half an hour later, Peter was ready to leave.

'Well, my dear family, it's time to go back home,' he suggested. 'After all this rain, the water level will be higher than normal, but I think I'll still be able to manage to get the coach and ourselves across the river, by using the bridge.'

The Henderson family picked up their belongings, after which everyone went outside, with both Martin and Sam coming to see them off.

'All the best of luck, dear honourable Hendersons, and please have a safe journey home,' Sam mentioned, before they departed.

'Thank you. It was a short but sweet visit,' Anna replied, giving a quick and cheeky wink to Sam, which he promptly returned to Anna with great mischievousness.

'Hey Sam, don't forget to come and visit my ferry. I'll be waiting for you when you're ready,' Peter reminded him and shook hands, as two gentlemen would.

Martin also wished them good luck, as he stood aside, waving them farewell.

Together, they rode in the carriage without talking for the majority of the trip. Anna finally broke the silence by remarking, 'they are a perfectly friendly family.'

'Yes, I think so too,' Peter replied, feeling a great sense of kinship with Martin and Sam.

It was very late when they arrived home, and the entire town was resting peacefully. Except for fighting cat and dog noises that could be heard somewhere in the distance, in the dead of night.

Anna's mother, Katherine, was already in bed fast asleep. Peter was tired and completely exhausted. As a result, he went directly to bed without any hesitation. Adrian, on the other hand, was still busily thinking about Sam's education and pondered about why it was taking such a long time for him to finish school. Adrian figured the poor man must be a terrible student, who kept on failing his exams miserably.

For Anna, the evening had been entirely glorious; as she experienced a variety of different feelings and expectations. She couldn't sleep and kept glancing at her snoring husband. She quietly left her bed so as not to wake Peter, walking to the window. She longingly looked outside into the dark, busily fantasising about being with Sam. It was well after midnight when she finally went to sleep. What she dreamt initially may have been about rain, mud, her dress, Peter, or what she had earlier eaten during the day. But her most expressive dream was when in deep sleep and clearly spoke, 'you are my idol. You are my hero. You are here with me now.'

Peter awoke to these words and believed his beloved wife was dreaming about him. 'Thank you, sweetie,' he grumbled, with his sleepy voice, hugging her.

CHAPTER 4

Master Adrian was a clever student and received many awards every year for his achievements.

'Mister and Mrs Henderson, your son is an excellent student! You know, if he continues to perform in the way he is now, you will in no time have a professor living with you under your roof,' Mrs Betsy commented, at this parent/teacher meeting.

Having received such exceptional compliments from their son's teacher, Peter and Anna were undoubtedly proud and happy. They also took great delight in boasting about Adrian's performance to anyone who would listen.

9

After a while, Peter again sought to organise some special time away from work with his family to celebrate. So, in advance, Peter first arranged it with his ferry assistant. Once done, he then went to Anna and informed her of his plan and why.

'My darling, on this coming Sunday, we should go out again somewhere, together. How does that sound?' he asked.

'Oh yes, why not, that suits me fine. Are we going by

ourselves or... I mean.' Anna thought about Sam, but realised it was best to just stop talking.

Having heard Peter, Adrian became hyper-excited at this new development to do something different. 'We're going out, oh boy, I so like your idea, Dad,' Adrian said eagerly.

'Yes, my son. We're going out, but the question is, where shall we go? Maybe we should go bush ...' Peter began to reply but was quickly stopped by his son.

'Oh no dad, not the bush, I want to go to the same place we were last time, at the waterfall. Can we please, please, pretty please,' he begged, with crossed arms.

His father noted the look of utter desperation on Adrian's face and suggested a reasonable compromise. 'Well, probably not exactly the same place but quite near.'

'Dad, no, that's not good enough. I want to go to exactly the same place where we were the very last time and nowhere else,' Adrian continued to demand.

Peter finally gave into his son's wishes, nodded in agreement and heartily hugged his son. 'Okay, okay, you've won, this time. We're going to the waterfall.'

'Oh wow. Thanks a million, dad. That's the place and nowhere else!' Adrian happily said.

He then turned to his wife. 'Anna, other than celebrating our son's educational achievements, I have another purpose for this planned outing,' Peter emphasised. At this, she widened her eyes and anxiously listened to what Peter had to say. 'In the next couple of days, I'll call Elena to come with us and have also considered inviting Sam to join us as well. What do you think of my grand master plan?'

'Oh yes, I like it a lot. Of course, Elena and Sam should come along for the ride. The more, the merrier, that's what I say. It will make it a great day for all of us,' she happily agreed, eyes lighting up so bright they could have brightened a dark room.

Anna was blissfully unaware of Peter's attempt at match-making, to get Elena and Sam together, in hopes it could develop into a blossoming romance between them. After all, they were both single and Peter thought Sam would be the perfect man for his sister. Maybe one day in the future, Sam could become Peter's brother-in-law.

However, Peter never made that phone call, sidetracked with other more important duties, but fate interceded on his behalf.

¶

As usual on every Sunday morning, Peter, Anna, Adrian, and Elena attended church. After Sunday Mass, Elena would regularly visit the church cemetery, to pay respect to her father.

On this particular day however, Martin and his son, Sam, also visited the church. Peter and Anna saw them earlier while inside. *Good, this is my golden opportunity,* Peter thought. Meanwhile, Anna's heart skipped a beat in anticipation of speaking to Sam again so soon after their last visit.

Adrian leaned in closer to his mother. 'Hey Mum, I see ronrom Sam is here,' he whispered, while shaking her arm.

'He is an agronomist, so please be quiet, Adrian,' she softly replied.

'Maybe or maybe not, but he must be really dumb if he's still at school!' Adrian commented, to which Anna could not respond.

9

After Sunday Mass had been conducted, the Henderson family stood outside, chatting with friends. Peter's eyes were restlessly searching for Martin and Sam. He finally saw them talking to a few people they knew.

'My dear family, excuse me for a second. I'm just going to speak with our new tenant and his son,' Peter casually mentioned before he went to join them.

'Oh, what a surprise, how are you?' Martin exclaimed when he saw his new friend approach.

'I'm fine. Is it possible for Sam to come now and briefly have a chat with us?' Peter asked of Martin.

'Of course, he can,' Martin replied as he answered Peter's question. He then turned to Sam. 'You go with Mister Henderson. I'll join you shortly,' he said.

Sam naturally believed that maybe Peter's charming wife wanted to talk with him. He also felt contented about the developing friendship between himself and Peter. As they got closer, Sam noticed a beautiful young girl he had not seen before. He wondered who she was.

'Elena, please meet Sam. He's the son of my new tenant and

he's here on holiday for five weeks only, while taking a break from his studies,' Peter said, as he introduced her.

'I am most pleased to meet you, sir,' Elena said politely and offered her hand to him.

Anna took a big breath to calm herself. The group had a small chat, during which Peter discussed his plan for the day.

'Because it's such a nice day, I'm thinking of going on a picnic with the family. We'd love to invite you Elena and Sam to come with us. What do you think? Would you like to join us for the afternoon?'

'That would be absolutely fine. I'm glad to accept your kind offer,' she said while subtly catching a glimpse at Sam.

'And I accept as well and look forward to being, in such stimulating company. And may I politely ask you Peter, when will we be leaving?' Sam asked.

'We can start right away. It's such a glorious Sunday with perfect weather, so obviously we can't miss the opportunity,' Peter responded.

In the meantime, Elena thought what a handsome young man Sam was. She remembered a suggestion her brother once made in the past: 'Elena, why not buy one of your own divine hats and who knows, you might nab yourself a handsome boyfriend.' She instinctively touched her hat while Sam continually glanced at her and smiled.

They all hurried back to their respective homes, to prepare themselves. Peter, Anna, and Adrian got ready and as prearranged. They went to collect Elena first and then visited the Martin's residence.

At Sam's place, while waiting with his father, he jokingly said to Peter upon his arrival, 'where were you? I've been waiting for such a long time. What sort of a schedule is this? There's no rain, no wind and you're still late!'

'Yes, Sam, I like your words. I know an agronomist is always on time,' Peter open-heartedly praised him. 'Can you imagine if someone, such as yourself, had none of those things to work with. What would become of the economy?'

'It would be total and utter chaos,' Sam said, joining in with the laughter as they walked towards the coach.

Peter and Sam sat in the front, while Elena and Anna sat behind. Master Adrian sat right at the back.

'Have a good time everyone, and God speed,' Martin wished and off they went.

As they were disappearing into the distance, Vivien rushed out with a tin filled with some homemade biscuits.

'Oh no, they left again so quickly. I wanted to give them some treats to have upon their journey, just in case they got a bit hungry,' she exclaimed with disappointment.

'Sorry, but you're too late. They were in a hurry, but it's not too late for us to eat. Let's go inside and have a bit of a munch with a well-earned cuppa,' he said, and so they did.

⸹

Peter took a different route towards their destination that was surrounded with spectacular scenery. They travelled through the forest, passed Peter's property on their right-hand side, over the little creek, and turned into a wide green valley. Far away was the place they wanted to visit.

As the horses galloped at a leisurely pace, Anna's mind was also attending to many painful speculations about Sam, Elena, and herself. She was deeply engaged in her own scheming, plotting and planning, that no one else would ever know about.

But Peter and Sam were chatting away amicably, and were occasionally caught laughing loudly. Suddenly, Peter turned around to ask something of Anna, but she was unaware of what had just been said.

In her confusion, she answered, 'what, to whom are you speaking? Can you please repeat yourself?' And so on with so many questions.

However, when Sam went to say something to the ladies, both Elena and Anna simultaneously asked if he was talking to them, while he understood the intention of both women. 'I'm sorry, ladies. From now on, I'll be sure to mention your names, so each of you will know who I am speaking to,' he said, chuckling to himself.

Damn Elena. She's going to win his heart, where I don't stand a chance, Anna thought jealously, great gushes of anger rising within her heart.

Little Adrian simply sat silently at the back of the coach, totally mesmerised at the turning spokes and tried to count how many times the wheel was spinning. 'Oh, dear waterfall, I'll be with you again real soon,' Adrian suddenly exclaimed. He planned in his head, all those things he wanted to do when he reached the place he loved so much, but no one paid any attention to his dreams.

A mental storm of uneasiness brewed in Anna's mind. She felt a relentless discomfort and finally was forced to ask Elena about her feelings for Sam.

'Elena, what do you think about him?' Anna whispered abruptly and completely out of the blue.

Elena didn't quite understand what she was asking, so merely blinked and replied. 'Who are you talking about?'

Anna gestured towards Sam.

'Well, he is a most handsome man,' she said to Anna, sure to lower her voice so the men driving in the front could not hear.

'Hmm!' Anna smiled, with pure and unadulterated anger.

Now, that's interesting. Why did Anna ask me about Sam? This most puzzling question continued to circulate through Elena's mind.

Anna ruthlessly bit her lip, vowing to keep quiet about the subject for the rest of the trip. But her heart betrayed her, pounding more vigorously with the growing sense of uneasiness and gloom.

9

At the wide emerald valley, they were surrounded with pleasant scenery. Endless chains of snow peaked mountains, heaps of tall brown rocks and scattered trees, with a large variety of birds who all sang their special songs. The constant sound of the horses' hooves and the rattling coach wheels, scaring wild rabbits into hiding. Peter was in high spirits, joyously encouraging the horses to speed up. Sam participated as well, goading him on.

'Peter, what would happen if the wheel of the coach fell off now?' he jokingly enquired.

'Ah, the wheels of a Henderson's carriage can never fall off,' he said reassuringly, whipping the horses harder and causing them to move even faster.

Adrian became quite excited. 'Dad, wow! This is so amazing! I love it. Go faster, don't slow down, go faster!' he said from the back.

Sam began to have a change of heart, as he noticed how Anna and Elena were becoming somewhat alarmed at the back.

'Peter, stop please. It's getting too dangerous,' Sam said, loudly raising his voice, so he may be heard over the noisy rumblings of the carriage crashing haphazardly over long rough tufts of grass and rocks, which caused Sam to hold onto his seat more firmly.

'Sam, I told you we are Henderson's! Those wheels were made during my grandfather's time and they are still working, as if they were only made yesterday. Good workmanship lasts forever, I can tell you,' Peter shouted, as he continued his wild ride across the rocky valley, holding everyone else hostage, except for his son who was a willing participant.

'Peter, slow down please! listen to Sam,' Anna screamed out in fear, believing her husband was going way too fast, but her words were not heard.

Adrian was overwhelmed with joy and suddenly announced, 'hey Dad, I see something dead ahead!'

He tried to warn his dad, but it was too late. The wheel

hit the protruding rock and the coach jumped high off the ground, swung from side to side a few times and came back down on the track with a heavy thud. Thankfully, nobody was injured; however, the incident was the major cause of a big scare for everyone on board.

'Oh hell, that was a close call. Thank the Lord we're all okay,' a frightened Peter shouted.

'Oh my God, what's happened? What did we hit?' pale-faced Elena asked.

Adrian was the only one who remained ignorant about the seriousness of the situation. 'Dad, Dad! That was so much fun. I flew high up into the sky. Wow, can you do that trick one more time, please?'

Peter was still in shock, so he didn't hear his son speaking to him.

'I'm so sorry folks. This was entirely my fault. I predicted it, and so it came to pass,' Sam said as he willingly took responsibility for the accident.

'Hey Dad, are we there yet?' Adrian asked with curiosity.

Because Peter was still too preoccupied with this unexpected mishap, again he could not answer his son. The event that just happened could very easily have proved fatal to some or all of his fellow passengers. People who had put their lives into Peter's hands to get them to where they were going safely.

For a while, nobody else could say anything either about the frightful disaster. Finally, they arrived, and everybody was greatly relieved as they stepped once again and onto solid ground.

'Oh my, how glorious,' Elena said in disbelief as she looked around. In the past, she had heard from other people about this place and now knew they were absolutely right.

'Yes, I totally agree with you, it's a very special place indeed,' Sam added, moving closer to Elena. 'These will be pleasant memories for me when I return to university.'

Anna became restless and walked closer to Sam, standing next to him on the other side. Anna politely asked Sam. 'Nice waterfall, isn't it?'

'So much water, so powerful… and yes, it truly is a magical place. How could anyone not like it?' he answered.

Peter stood near the coach and horses, unloading the picnic gear.

Adrian while playing, went too close to the fast running water. Anna noticed and warned him, 'Please, don't go too close, Adrian. It's dangerous!'

Adrian did not take her warning at all seriously, wondering what she meant. He looked around for this 'dangerous' thing, but could not find it. So, he dismissed the idea altogether and continued playing. Occasionally, he would look to the top of the waterfall where a big rock stood. He could not deny the urge any longer, so went to his mum and explained.

'Mum, if I go to the top of the waterfall and stand on it, I will become big as well. Everyone will be able to see me, so they'll know who I am. The people will be able to hear me, so they could listen and do as I say. Oh, it would be so grand to do this!'

Anna was taken aback at her son's words. 'No dear, that's just your imagination. None of what you speak of can ever happen. It's a child's stupid dream,' she said, trying desperately to convince him.

Adrian simply waved her off and walked away. His mind was set: he wanted to know more, and made his way over to Peter instead.

'Dad, what else is on top of the waterfall apart from the rock?' he asked inquisitively.

To make Adrian happy, Peter created a fictional story. 'Up there, stands an invisible glass house. If you go into this house, you become invisible as well.'

Peter thought his son would be satisfied with this answer, but Adrian was determined and continued to probe him with further questions. 'Dad, if you go into that invisible house, can you become a king?'

'Oh son, people say that any wish you have will come to pass if you're inside that house,' Peter replied, knowing the story was a bit too good to be true.

'Wow, this is so amazing, Dad. When I become king in my glass house and call for you, will you come to me?' Adrian excitedly enquired of his father.

'Of course, son,' Peter responded to fuel Adrian's happiness even further. What harm could come from doing so? 'Now go, run off and play.'

Adrian did as he was told.

❡

Peter untied the horses from the carriage and allowed them to graze. He fondly noticed that Elena and Sam were walking together with a cane basket, picking wild flowers while laughing and talking freely. They seemed to be relaxed in each other's company, and Peter quietly mused that they would make a lovely couple.

Meanwhile, Anna sat on a picnic blanket all alone, desperately trying to gather herself. She could not dismiss her feelings for Sam. She kept debating whether she was falling in love with him. He is indeed a most striking and debonair young man. The woman who would marry him would be very lucky, as he was most clever, educated, and charming. Surely, he must be an expert lover too. *If I was single, surely, he would be mine.*

She quickly attempted to bring herself back from her wicked thoughts, imagining what Sam may be thinking about her. More than likely, she was a married woman with a devoted husband and son. No way could he ever be her lover. Or he may be thinking she was an experienced woman and knew how to make a man feel special. *Or maybe, he just loves my company and nothing more?*

She then turned her mind to the possibility of Sam and Elena becoming a couple. *Sure enough, Elena is single, but she is too naive to have a boyfriend, and from a man's perspective, this would make her unapproachable to some degree. Elena is scattered, wild, and good for nothing; Sam is definitely not for her. She is wild.*

Elena grabbed and shook Anna out of her fantasies. 'Anna, who is wild? Do you mean the flowers?'

'Oh yes. Elena, the wild bird that just flew overhead,' Anna replied in confusion as she pointed her finger towards a fine feathered friend in the sky, which wasn't there.

Elena became puzzled at her response. She had been talking about flowers, not birds. While Sam thought that surely, Peter's wife was living a double life.

Chapter 5

While everyone else was playing, talking, and having a lovely time at the picnic, Anna simply sat and kept analysing her life. Her mind drifted back to a conversation she had with her mum recently.

'Mother dearest, I was more fortunate when we were living on our own property. Then I felt… oh, I don't know what I'm trying to say.'

'But Anna, you are at my place and you've got everything here you need, because I'm helping you,' Katherine replied in dismay.

'Yes Mother, it looks like that, but it's not the same … I mean …' she stuttered.

'Oh, my dear Anna, everything changes, and we shouldn't be negative about life, only positive. Listen, my daughter, I do understand you very well. Peter has a job on the ferry every day till late at night. Sometimes he's at work for even longer hours, for many days in a row. And it can be extremely demanding to adjust to this sort of routine if you're trying to create a normal family life at home as well. On top of that, you have Adrian and he has to be taken to and from school each day. Those times I know are particularly hardest for you.

Also, to be at home by yourself can be quite boring sometimes and that's why I suggest you find someone special that you have a connection with and to spend quality time with them. By doing so, this will change your perceived boring life into something much more enjoyable.'

But Anna selectively remembered only the bit of her mother's advice, which emphasised the need to 'find someone!' In her mind, this 'someone' had to be no other than Sam. And he was emerging as quite a handsome catch. She continued to try and pull her scattered mind in some sort of order, but had some difficulty in doing so.

My Peter is a hardworking man, so he doesn't have time for me anymore. I can't live like this anymore. I need and deserve a real man, she thought to herself.

Had Peter noticed that Anna behaved differently towards him and even if he had, could he change anything? He had been working on the ferry for quite a long time before Anna chose to visit Peter at his workplace. She only did it the once, because she was simply not interested. She mentioned to her husband at the time, 'that's the job and tradition of the *Henderson family,* not mine.'

She was so deeply submerged in her thoughts that she barely noticed Adrian asking her for food, but found enough energy within her being to answer her son. 'Oh yes, of course, we are going to have a picnic lunch soon.'

While answering Adrian, she was busy looking around for the whereabouts of Elena and Sam. Anna soon found them further down at the field, holding hands and talking. After calming Adrian, she laid back down on the rug.

Anna tried to convince herself that Sam did not love Elena. She tried to think about what love was. *Is love a primitive experience, hot, cold, or a massive sham? Maybe Sam's body is there in the field, but his mind could be elsewhere- at university, at home, in the tavern, with prostitutes? Maybe he has a fulltime girlfriend in London? Oh Lord, there are so many questions but one thing I know for sure is... Sam is mine and no one else's.*

If my Peter knew what I was thinking, he might say, 'Anna, what's wrong? Am I not enough for you?' Or he might say, 'So what, I too am thinking about a nice girl. Yes. Everyone is free to think as they wish,. There is no law against it. Or he might just leave me alone if he has somebody on his ferry. Oh Lord, please forgive me. Did I commit a sin by thinking this way?

She fell further into a state of high anxiety when she imagined what other people would say if they saw her with Sam. She heard their cruel voices in her mind. *Look at that damn Anna. She has already found a lover and is hiding away in secret places... only to satisfy her uncontrollable lust. She is nothing but a cheap street woman of the night. The man looks like a real scumbag too. What is Anna thinking? She is such a disgrace to our small town.*

She then began to imagine the old men with their walking sticks, hearing aids, and thick glasses, limping up to knock on her door and pleading, *'We... we... heard that you are... one of them. Can we come in?'* What if they dropped dead on her doorstep? Her thoughts were like a cyclone as they blustered from one extreme to another. *Let the townspeople think what they want. They were born to chat and gossip. They make a* mountain out of every mole hill. *They are dishonest too. Nothing good can come from these types of accusations, so damn them all.* And although she tried to be logical, she still could not control her jealousy.

Yes, all in all, I have a right to Sam. He is on my property. That vulgar Elena can only dream about him. I am not ashamed. Hers is soon to come, but my shame has long passed. This is a big advantage in being an exceptional lover. She laughed loudly, and then in her imagination, spoke to her sister-in-law. *Elena, you're an extremely dull person. You look okay on the outside, but inside, you're like a rotting, worm-infested stump. You don't deserve a man. You still haven't got the body for him; your legs, bust, bottom, mouth. Go, go from my mind!* But Elena was not to be banished so easily.

I will take revenge on her. What does the little slut have that attracts Sam so much? Absolutely nothing and compared to me, she rates a big fat zero. Oh, if I should find her alone, I will pluck her hair, bash her, blister her eyes, force her to eat dirt, and throw her into a swine pit. That is her rightful place, not with Sam. She can eat slop instead of having his kiss.

When Sam asks, 'who is this dirty pig-like creature?' I will respond by saying, 'My darling Sam, this is your stinking bitch.' Can't you see how this disgusting animal is trying to seduce you? Sam, please, wake up and realise what you are doing. I'm here with you. I can help you forget all about her. Oh, my darling Sam, come to me, please. I will make you happy and satisfied. Sam, I can easily take you to a heavenly paradise. We will live in the Garden of Eden. We will enjoy flowers, fruits, and the smell of nature. This is also the same place where Adam and Eve were born naked. They walked, talked, laughed, and made love together, forever. You can be Adam and I'll be Eve. What could be better than that? Sam, my heart won't lie to you. You were born for me. You are mine and only mine. No one else can have you.

Experiencing great mental anguish, Anna continued to lie on the picnic blanket, with eyes tightly closed and her erratic mind wandering.

Very quietly, Elena and Sam finally approached Anna with flowers in their hands. Sam indicated to Elena for the need of complete silence, putting his finger to his mouth. Elena simply nodded and walked away as Sam gently placed a flower on top of Anna's forehead.

Startled away from her tortured longings, Anna spoke the last thing she'd been thinking. 'Oh yes… yes, you are mine and no one else can have you!' she breathily whispered. Upon awakening to the present moment, she bolted upright and corrected herself.

'Oh, it's you, I thought …' But she could not find a reason to continue the sentence.

Sam simply gave Anna a knowing smile. She noticed that Peter and Adrian were nowhere to be seen.

'Anna, this time you look flushed and full of happiness,' Sam mentioned with intensity.

Anna felt greatly relieved. 'Where's Elena?' she asked Sam, hoping for some precious moments alone with him.

'She went to bring some drinks,' Sam replied, pointing towards the coach.

The genuine display of fine behaviour and caring attitude further enhanced Anna's delusion about Sam and his feelings about her.

She'd incorrectly concluded that he loved her, how they would later become engaged and married. Anna wished for Sam to continue speaking nice words, and couldn't stop thinking about desiring him.

Peter, Adrian, and Elena finally made their way over to Sam and Anna.

'Oh well, I think it's about time that we have some lunch!' Peter mentioned.

Everybody sat and partook in a tasty meal together of crusty homemade bread, fried chicken, scones with jam and cream, sponge cake, tea, and homemade lemonade.

After a while, Peter and young Adrian decided to go for a lengthier stroll.

'Well son, we can now walk for however long you wish. Am I right?' Peter said, patting his full and satisfied stomach.

'Yes Dad, let's go,' Adrian cheerfully exclaimed.

Sam, Elena, and Anna decided to stay and enjoy each other's company instead.

'Later, we'll go for a walk too. It would be a smart way to burn off the weight gained from eating all this fine food,' Sam mentioned to Peter just before he left with his son.

After the meal, Anna kept pumping her mind with imaginary conversations she would like to have with Sam. *Why are you so quiet? Say something: I want to listen to some more of your compliments. Talk to me, please. Do you hear my thoughts and feel the love I have? I so strongly feel a burning passion for you, but you're just sitting there, like an unresponsive blob of a jellyfish, without saying a word to me. You're a fully-grown man, so please speak up, so we can have a proper conversation. Please Sam, do as I want, and I'll give in return such physical and lustful love that will make you forget all about your studies- where you won't ever wish to return to university. Why do you need study when you can be loved by me instead? Remember Sam, today we live, tomorrow we die! Are you ashamed of me? Oh, don't worry, my darling, if you're ashamed in love, then I will teach you how to love. Yes, Sam, the shame you're experiencing now is but a monument of the past for me. Yes, it is the truth.*

Anna fought tooth and nail to restrict the torrent of her wicked imaginings, a battle of which she was losing.

Oh Sam, I love Peter, but you are my hero and that's the main difference between him and you. Each time I look upon your face, I wish I could kiss you. Your secret seductive smile hiding behind your sexy moustache is what I crave and can't resist! I wish I could get more of you. My Sam, please move a bit closer and leave that worthless vagabond, Elena, alone. Do it right no…, come on. Don't even think about trying to kiss her. If you do, I shall have to tear her apart, from limb to limb.

This was when Peter arrived back to the picnic site with Adrian, drinking a refreshing glass of water and sat to catch his breath. His young son played close by, having a happy time at their place of tranquility.

'Sam, my good friend, what do you think about this place? Do you like it?' Peter asked, with interest.

'Oh yes, I do like it very much. I wouldn't mind coming here more often. I am having a most enjoyable time,' Sam replied, feeling unimpeded from the pull of normal life.

Anna's desires were starting to kick into action, and she slowly moved her finger to touch Sam's hand. Completely bewildered, Sam quickly moved his hand away.

Oh, Sam! Touch me, please. There's no need to withdraw, Anna thought with a deep breath and with a newfound courage, she went to make physical contact with him again. *What harm could it do?*

At this second attempt, Sam glanced at her and read her mind immediately. He was beginning to grasp the full intensity of Anna's real desires. However, so as not to arouse Peter's suspicion, he did not respond to her touch.

From the first time since meeting her, Sam knew what Anna wanted. However, he pretended to remain unaware, in order to keep himself focused upon his studies. As Sam first began his university degree, he remembered the sincere promise he made to his parents and to himself: his study must always come first, and women could come later. He was trying not to get entangled in love and drama, with all the unnecessary implications this may bring.

When he made this solemn vow to himself and his parents, he never figured on ever meeting someone like Anna. Yet, here he was, now caught in uncertainty about his relationship with this most desirable married woman.

Chapter 6

That particular day created lasting memories for all concerned. The shift in paradigm of everyone's thoughts, feelings and memories added significance to the outstanding location. It was as if each individual had formed, or lost, a connection with each other.

Elena wasn't sure if she would ever experience such a wonderful and most exciting day again. Meeting Sam was the first time she had this level of close interaction with a young man, and her wayward feelings spiraled into emotions of love.

Anna, an experienced and married woman, already has someone to love, but still wished for more, her intrinsic lust is not satisfied by her husband.

Sam, a single young gentleman, arrived at Plymouth on a vacation with plans to return to university to continue his studies. His vacation was only last for a short time.

Peter was everyone's caring host, serving, talking and trying his best to create a favourable impression on everyone present.

§

As the minutes flew into hours and the morning turned to afternoon, everyone was ready to return home.

'Well what can I say dear friends, it's time for us to head back,' Peter said, as he started loading the carriages for the return journey. 'If I was a magician, I'd stop this day indefinitely, but unfortunately, I can't.'

Everyone assisted Peter in loading the carriages and sat in the same positions.

Adrian was a little disappointed and began to sulk. 'I know I'll be the king one day and everybody will then be forced to listen to my words,' he declared. However, in the commotion of people and noise of the coach, nobody heard what the young boy said.

'You know what, Peter? I could stay in this beautiful place forever,' Sam enthusiastically announced on their travels home.

'Yes Sam, you're right. It has that effect on many people, when they come to visit this magical place. And if you should choose to live here, you would become our immediate neighbour,' Peter quipped, halfheartedly. 'You see, my Anna already has plans for building our new home right on this very same spot, isn't that right, dear?'

He turned to catch a glimpse of her when she did not respond to his question. Instead, she sat still like a statue, eyes shut, staring without thinking.

Meanwhile, Adrian kept repeating to himself, 'I will be the big king. I will be the invisible big king in the glass house, I will.'

❡

It was late in the evening, when they arrived to drop Sam off.

Elena was visibly happy with the company she'd kept, and left a strong and lasting influence on Sam. He leaned closer to her.

'Thanks so much for making my day so great. The picnic was most enjoyable and wish you well, dear Elena,' he said with a smile and a wink.

Anna had not witnessed or heard what just happened between Elena and Sam, as she was so overwhelmed with the power of her own painful thoughts.

'See you sometime soon, Sam,' Peter remarked before leaving to drop off Elena.

But before he could say anything further, Elena spoke up. 'Don't worry about me, Peter. My house is not far, so I can easily walk back home from here.'

'Oh no, my dear sister, you can't walk that far. Aren't you tired?' he replied.

'No, Peter, I feel more rested than ever. As well as this, my own happiness has given me a new spurt of energy, which I didn't know I had before,' she stated.

'Hmm, well if you say so,' Peter said, realising what his sister was really trying to say about Sam. He left her in his trusting and safe hands.

When Peter, Anna, and Adrian arrived home, Katherine was still awake, sitting with contentment in her chair, reading an historical romance novel.

On the contrary, Adrian was exhausted and dropped off to sleep straight away, having not gathered enough strength to even say his nightly prayers.

'How was the picnic?' Anna's mother asked with interest.

'Good,' Anna replied.

'For me, it was more than just good,' Peter cheerfully added.

'I'm so pleased it went well for all of you,' Anna's mother replied.

Over the next few days, restless Anna had berserk impressions of Sam. Since that eventful, life changing day, her mind was broken, and so performed her duties in a dazed, unusual manner. Her mother noticed and commented on her condition.

'Anna dear, I've noticed you've been overly pensive for the past couple of days, that maybe you're experiencing some difficult feelings. Tell me, what is it? Do you feel sick?' she gently asked.

'Mother, everything is fine. It's just a slight headache, that's all. Nothing more,' she said.

'A headache! Oh dear, go to bed and relax until it's time to get Adrian from school,' she suggested.

'Oh, Mother, you don't know what kind of burden I've been carrying within my heart...' Anna quietly mentioned. In a flurry of bewilderment, she began asking personal questions about her mother's own youth and love life. 'You too were young once. Did you ever feel ...'

But she dared not continue with that particular line of questioning. Anna left her mother alone to be in peace.

Hmm, my poor daughter, Katherine thought. Maybe Peter's job is taking its toll on their marriage, along with needing to cope with the daily needs of Adrian, them renting their home out to complete strangers and other reasons…

§

During the passing of time, Anna's thoughts were becoming messily entrenched into a web of lies and deceit. Knowingly, she could sense it was about to drop her into a deep hole of destruction, but felt powerless to stop it. The worst part was she knew that she was the only one to blame for what was about to unfold.

Oh Lord, what should I do? Who will stop me from falling into this bottomless pit? Only Sam can save me. Sadness, lust, and love fills my heart. What do I do- run, stand, wait, wail or sing?

'Go to him Anna! you must,' she heard a voice whisper from within her soul, and so gave in, surrendering to this suggestion.

Yes, yes, I should go. I will go and be with Sam. Oh, who is going to give me what I have lost? My darling Sam- and not Peter, will give me what I desire and deserve.

Unable to handle the mental and emotional pressure she placed upon her own shoulders, Anna prepared to go alone to visit Sam. She wanted to be with him, to talk to him, and to feel his presence. She started to dwell on the never ending internal questions running rampant inside her head. *Will he talk to me with pleasant words or ugly words? Will he say, 'what exactly do you want from me?' Or, it could be even worse if he said, 'you're an ugly old hag. Get away from me, you bitch.'*

But she happily deluded herself by imagining a more

positive outcome. *Sam could say, 'my darling Anna, please come. I want to kiss you in a way you'll never forget. I want to rip your clothes off and give you twenty-five sugar cane smacks upon your baby-smooth bottom.'* On these occasions, she enjoyed visualising Sam touching her naked skin.

¶

This is when Anna unexpectedly remembered standing at the altar on her wedding day, where she promised Peter she would remain faithful to him forever. But now, she felt the same for Sam, and in the eyes of God, that made her an adulterer. Even though nothing happened yet in a physical sense, it had already happened many times in her head.

Pulled back from her past, Anna could see and hear Adrian crying out for her and tried to ignore his needs and pleas. All those feelings for Sam were temporarily thrown away, and she stood silently, watching them vanish into thin air.

She kept thinking about one thing only: how would all this end? *The rich people living on the hill always regarded us as being a most fortunate and respectable family. If those same snotty-nosed people knew the truth, they might say, 'this is a complete disaster. What an ugly and horrid affair it has been.'*

Not liking this particular train of discourse, Anna abruptly eradicated it: *those types of people are just your typical gossips. That they are jealous of me, but I don't care. Let them tattle-tale all they want. Until their viper tongues fall off, and they no longer speak wicked evil!*

No matter what, I will go to Sam- fabricate a story for his benefit as to why I am there, unaccompanied by my husband. But what will happen if Peter later finds out what I've done? He may throw me out of our home, straight into Hell, and then firmly slam the door shut in my face. Anna kept contemplating hundreds of questions and possible outcomes, but only time could answer her ponderings.

While inwardly conversing with herself, Anna stood like a zombie next to the window. Automatically waving to someone she didn't even know. At that moment, her mother entered the room with hot tea and cake on a tray, which she placed upon the table before them.

Katherine believed her darling daughter was not herself. *She's changed somehow, terribly distraught about something or someone.*

'Anna, sit and have some tea. You'll feel better if you do.'

Anna, grateful for a reprieve from her internal churnings, walked towards her mother and hugged her tightly, never wanting to let go.

❡

The following day was cold, windy, and overcast. Anna took a deep breath and told herself, *this is it. Today is **the** day I visit Sam, unannounced.*

With growing excitement, she jumped out of bed, took a shower, combed her hair neatly and wore a beautiful dress which showed a generous amount of cleavage for Sam to admire. She added some splashes of expensive perfume on the nape of her neck, made Adrian his breakfast, and got him ready for school.

'Mum, you look especially lovely today,' Adrian commented.

'Thank you,' she replied as if on auto-pilot, still thinking about the journey she was undertaking shortly after taking her son to school.

'Anna, it looks as if you're dressed for a special occasion. Going somewhere?' her mother asked politely.

'Oh no, I just plan to drop Adrian off to school as per usual and then do a bit of shopping in town,' replied Anna.

'You don't look so well. Please look after yourself. The day is overcast, and it might rain. So be a good girl and take an umbrella with you,' her mother reminded Anna.

'I'm … I'm alright now, there's no need for alarm,' Anna replied with growing annoyance.

Katherine wasn't so sure.

Without a second glance or explanation, Anna took her leather handbag and left. She hurriedly dropped Adrian to school and with renewed eagerness, started towards their rental property in order to visit Sam.

Will I see him? Will he be home? He might be anywhere- in town, walking around without a care in the world… or he could be with that scoundrel Elena. Anna blushed, breathless and distracted. She kept riding and finally reached her destination. This is when a new question was brought forward to the forefront of her mind. *What will happen when I see Sam?*

Suddenly, she lost all confidence, and a strange concoction of emotions mixed with an unexplainable fear, overwhelming her. She couldn't understand what happened to the same confidence she'd had when first starting out on her mission today!

What now? What should I do? What will I say? She then forced herself to regain her composure. *No, no, I can't go backwards, only forward. Yes, I want to see him. I am a woman, he is a man and we have lots in common. I love him so.*

Because this was the first time Anna was visiting the rental property without her husband, she was feeling pressure. She felt an unexpected surge of warmth with memories about Peter, the way in which he could converse with everyone about anything. His interests ranged from kitchen dishes, agricultural products, and even abnormal weather patterns in the sky. Anna admired his ease of communication with people, a quality he'd developed particularly through his work at the ferry. That type of mundane discussion was never really her cup of tea. It appeared to be all too superficial and boring, but at times like this, she had to admit it came in handy.

Anna suddenly found she was in an abnormally different situation from what she is normally comfortable with. Showing no interest in erecting fences or tractor work, she tried to find an excuse for what she really wants to talk to Sam about.

Through her strong emotions of love, Anna felt as if she could undergo a personality shift and begin talking with authority, like a judge, professor, solicitor, or even a horse racing broadcaster. In critical moments, she knew she had the ability to change and adapt to whatever is required.

After a long pause, she took a breath, stepped off the coach and tidied her hair before knocking on the door, but nobody answered.

'Anybody home?' she softly enquired.

Feeling nervous, she squeezed her handbag tightly, coughing in the hopes of drawing attention to herself. She knocked again a bit harder, and that is when she discovered the door had not been closed properly.

Hmm, it's open, she realised, and went inside to investigate further. *Oh Lord! Where is he?*

Anna looked around and wasn't sure whether to wait, sit, or search for somebody. Why was he not home? She looked for a place to put her handbag and as she turned, she saw Sam behind her, standing near the threshold.

She jumped on the spot, as if she had just received an electric shock. 'Oh my, you … you scared me!'

'Well, well! What a nice surprise. Please accept my apology for scaring you, but I thought it was my father who had returned. But may I also say, you're most welcome to visit here anytime that you wish,' he casually mentioned, quite unaffected by her reaction towards him.

She simply gazed as he continued watching her intensely.

'Have you come by yourself? Where's your husband?'

'Yes Sam, I have come alone. Peter's working on the ferry today and I … just happen to be here, but he may possibly visit later.'

'Ah yes, I understand,' he said, as he approached her. 'Well Anna, again it's nice to see you and tell me, what is your news?' he asked, while smiling at her.

'Sam, I was passing by and … and remembered I may be lost …'

'You think you're lost?' he asked with a laugh.

'No, not me, silly,' Anna hastily added, with a giggle. 'I meant to say that, I think… I've lost my brooch somewhere here.'

'A brooch?' he wondered.

'Yes, my brooch,' she said. 'It's a valuable family heirloom given to me by my grandmother and has great sentimental value.'

'Oh, well … that's most unfortunate then,' he replied, unsure of how else to respond.

'I must have lost it last time my family and I were here. I really don't know what's happened to it?' she lied, showing visible signs of pretend disappointment.

'Yes, yes, it could be here,' he mentioned. 'My parents may have found your brooch and kept it in a safe place that I don't know about. I hope this is the case and if so, when they come home, we will return it to you at the first available opportunity.'

Anna just discovered that Sam is indeed at home by himself. *Hmm, my golden opportunity should not be missed!* She thought Sam was simply acting unaware of the real purpose of her visit, even though he knew precisely what she wanted.

'Please take a seat, Anna, before you fall down. You're looking kind of pale, my dear, with all the distress you must be under,' Sam suggested kindly, indicating a chair close to her. She drifted to it in an enchanted state and felt as though she would do anything he asked. She wondered about what would happen next?

'Why don't I make some coffee and then we can talk about everything,' he proclaimed. 'Please excuse me for a moment, my lady. I won't be too long.'

'Sam, can I help you? I know how to do it,' she said as she stood up.

'Oh no, you are my guest. Please sit and take the weight off your feet,' he replied, firmly holding her shoulder and easing her back into a sitting position.

'Let me do it, I'll make our coffees. How does that sound?' he questioned, giving Anna a cheeky wink. She was elated by his gestures and mannerisms.

'Oh, alright then,' she exclaimed as Sam left to prepare the hot drinks. While waiting, she pinched her cheeks to look more healthy and fresh, mended her hair, and readjusted her protruding bust a few times to be even more enticing and appealing than before.

§

He called out from the kitchen in the hopes she might join him there. 'Oh, Lady Henderson, how sweet and aromatic this coffee's going to be- exactly what we both want and need.'

Instead of hearing the word 'aromatic', Anna heard him say the coffee would be 'romantic.'

'This is what you want, isn't it?' he asked a second time, in a teasing manner.

She thought to herself, *for heaven's sake, Sam, that's why I've come to see you.*

Soon after, Sam arrived back from the kitchen. 'And now, my lady, we have to be careful not to burn ourselves. The coffee is extremely hot,' he mentioned, carefully putting the tray on a little table sitting between them.

'Oh, Sam, thank you so much for this,' she said, somewhat puzzled at him stating the obvious. *Perhaps he is nervous too.*

They sat together, gratefully sipping their drinks, looking at each other and thinking what to say next. From time to time, she touched her neck and chest, remembering her lost brooch. *I know he sees what I do, but he's trying hard to ignore all the signals.*

Sam felt most comfortable, while Anna remained eager, speechless, and waiting for some action. Sam suddenly and spontaneously burst into laughter, spilling hot coffee onto his trousers.

In shock, she widened her eyes and stared at him in disbelief! *What happened? Was he laughing at me?* she wondered with amazement.

'Excuse me, dear lady. Please accept my sincere apology about my unexpected laughter and spilling the coffee,' he said after a while, bent over, and wiped the coffee off his pants. 'Oh yes, it's an awful memory I just had.'

'And which memory is that?' she quickly asked in dismay.

'It's quite funny, really. I recalled once at university when my friend was drinking some coffee and to his horror, he found a button inside the cup,' Sam mentioned, shaking his head.

'Good Lord! How did it come to be there?' she asked with wonder.

'Yes well, that was the real hilarious bit, because he had it in his mouth and started chewing, only to realise it was a button! Somebody had played a practical prank on him. While in mixed company, anything can happen,' he said.

After hearing this story, she put her cup on the table. 'Oh, dear me, I didn't know something like that could ever happen,' she said out loud, sighed and shook her head.

'Anna, you are a clever, understanding, and sweet woman. You can easily judge what's right or wrong, but please don't think you'll find your brooch in the cup you just put down,' he joked.

'Yes Sam, I do believe you,' she replied in a hypnotic state, smiling at him.

'That's what I want from you: happy and above all, trustful. Now we can start the real serious talk. So please tell me, how's your family?'

'Everyone is good. As I mentioned before, Peter is attending to the ferry, while my sons at school and…' she replied, leaving the rest hanging in mid-air.

'Yes, I am well aware you've come to see me,' he quickly replied.

Anna opened her mouth to respond, but could not. He had caught her completely off guard.

In order to change the conversation further, he quickly stated. 'We had such a wonderful picnic near the waterfall. I'll never forget it, but did you like it as well?' Although, he already knew what she was going to say.

'Yes, Sam, I liked it a lot. I only wished the day never needed to end. Very soon if possible, I'd so love to live there for the rest of my life,' Anna said with pure joy in her eyes.

He stood a few times, walked around the room, came within touching distance. He gently squeezed her hand and asked, 'Anna, do you want some more?'

'Oh yes, Sam, of course I want…' she whispered with half

closed eyes, but could not continue with her sentence whilst he was at such close range, holding her hand.

'Do you want more coffee?' he asked, buying himself some more valuable play time, same way a cat would enjoy teasing a defenceless mouse.

'Coffee, oh yes. More coffee please, yes. Thank you,' she replied, tongue tied all of a sudden.

'Did anyone ever tell you that you have such soft hands?' Sam asked enticingly, just inches away from her face. He then looked and saw a ring that she was wearing. 'Is this your wedding ring?'

'Yes, Peter- I mean Sam!' she whispered in ecstasy, while she looked at his hands holding hers and thinking how wonderful it would be if they could hold her close, forever.

'Well Anna, I am at home alone. I am everything, host, stranger, and...'

'And a real man!' she blurted out all of a sudden, looking desirously into his hazel green eyes.

'Yes, and that too.' He could no longer resist and with some slight hesitation, kissed her luscious, wanton lips.

Anna's body exploded with pleasure in that special moment when he kissed her for the first time. She was not herself any more, but a slave to her endless desire and lust for Sam. Her heart started thumping so erratically and so loud, it felt as if it would jump out of her chest in sheer delight.

For Sam, the kiss was light and feathery, and lasted for only a small micro-second of time. No big deal for him. For Anna though, it was huge and an endless, heavenly experience! In her entire twenty-eight years of being married to Peter, she had never been emotionally lifted so high.

Oh, my dream is finally coming true, Anna thought as she happily gave a sigh of contentment. In order to still her mind of strong feelings, she went outside for some air. As she did so, she accidentally hit the wall instead of walking through the door.

Sam stood next to her, like a furnace burning at full blast. From this moment on, she didn't know where she had come from, where she was going, and what would happen next. It all remained a mystery to her, and she was fine with that.

'Sam, I'm here for you. Do you feel me? Do you want me?' she uttered and did not hear a reply, but certainly could still sense him, holding her close as she shut her eyes. All sense of time stopped, as they stood there in the room together.

¶

Later, in sheer and utter bliss, they heard a large flock of birds fly over the house, breaking the magic spell of their sweet dreams. Sam continued to whisper sweet love in Anna's ears, while they openly lied together naked in his bed, wishing this enjoyable liaison would continue forever. Anna then suddenly realised the full extent of what had transpired.

'Sam, oh Sam, I love you,' she kept repeating.

'Anna, it is fact. It did happen, but you can't love me,' he firmly said.

'It's a bit late for you to tell me that now, as you're all mine and I am yours,' she raised her voice, so he could absorb her words better and not reject them.

'Anna, please understand that you're a married woman. You have a family that you are responsible for and-'

'That's not important, Sam. I love you,' she interrupted him, not wanting to hear the rest of the ugly truth.

'Anna, let's be realistic. It's impossible for us to be together. I mean, you're a married woman with a young child who needs you,' he said, trying to convince her.

'Oh Sam, I am yours and I want you to be my husband,' she begged him.

'Oh Anna, I love you too, but I'm still single. I need more time, to decide what it is that I want long term,' he desperately requested.

'Sam, from now on, nothing can stop us from being together. I've been waiting forever, for this moment, ever since we first met. And yes, I do have a husband, but you are far better than him.'

He didn't know what to say to that last comment about Peter, so Sam stuck to the safer option. 'Oh, Anna please, it's true you have given me the best lovemaking session of my life. You are a desirable and most beautiful woman I've ever met,' he said, trying to soften her resolve.

'So then, what are you waiting for? Let's get married,' she replied, pulling no punches.

'Oh, dear Lord, it's not that easy, as you may think. I'm still studying. Besides which, I have never once thought about marriage,' he said, while unwillingly pushing her away.

'Sam please, don't talk like that,' she said sharply.

'Anna, I request you give me some breathing space to think about it, till next time we meet?' he requested.

'Sam, there'll be no next time. I can't love Peter anymore. We loved each other in the beginning, but then he abandoned me when he went to work on the ferry and, so we became estranged. All throughout our marriage, I never once faltered. I always remained a faithful wife, but Sam, I need a full-time husband, who is willing to be man enough to fulfil my needs. A man like you, do you understand me?' Anna questioned.

'I understand perfectly, but Anna, Peter is still your husband,' Sam reminded her as gently as he could.

'What's the difference if he is my husband or somebody else's?' she queried.

'Anna dear, I don't think we can be so rash about this sort of thing,' he hastily replied.

'To fall in love with each other, is that what you wanted to say?' she quickly added, as she hugged and kissed him hard. Anna then did an about flip in personality and started treating Sam as if he was her son. '

Oh Sam, Mummy loves you so much. I can smack you on the bum, kick, hug, scratch, and bite you. And even pull your spectacular moustache.' With that said, she roughly yanked out several hairs at the one time.

'Ouch, that hurt. Stop it,' he yelped like a hurt little puppy. He pushed her away, which didn't stop her for long.

'Oh, your mummy truly loves the hair which covers your face and body, my handsome young boy.' And then happily ripped a handful of hair from his chest.

'Holy hell woman, what are you trying to do, murder me until I give in to your demands?' he admonished.

'Just shut up. You're my little boy and you need to listen with respect while your mother speaks,' she said while hugging and caressing him with butterfly kisses all over his body. 'I love you, Sam. You know what that means don't you?'

'Yes, I know,' he said, as he stole a quick glance at the wall clock.

'Then tell me, what does it mean?' she replied.

'It's all about love,' he answered.

'Not just love Sam, but *true* love. There is a difference between the two.'

From this moment on, Anna was marked with a loss of guilt and shame. Only a short while ago, Anna accepted he was merely a stranger and now she knew that Sam belonged to her. She was so glad she came.

¶

Anna was also aware that one day, Sam would go back to university and leave her with nothing more than fond memories of a brief love affair which could never last, leaving Anna with a broken heart. What would she do without him? Her most painful concern was wondering if he loved her only long enough to have her in his bed. These thoughts surged through her whirling mind. She took responsibility for being the instigator of this illegal liaison, but at the same time, she also knew she could take revenge if he forced her hand.

Still in bed, the two lovers were individually thinking about how they got themselves into this mess, which they rushed into without giving any consideration to the future ramifications of their actions.

This is my property Sam. You have come to me and not the other way 'round, she could hear herself saying, and then chose to rethink that plan of action. *No, no, I can't say that. I need him more than he needs me!*

She noted to herself that Sam had nothing to lose. Any moment, he could pack his belongings and leave for good. For all she knew, he could spit on her and refer to her as being a typical heartless bitch. Who knows, maybe they would both cheat on each other on their own terms.

After blissfully lying in bed together, they started to make a move to get dressed.

'Anna, we're now going to have to look for your lost brooch. Am I right?' he reminded her.

'Ah, my darling Sam, whoever really lost their brooch, let them look for it instead,' she smiled and started kissing him again.

He grinned and enjoyed another forbidden, golden moment with her.

'And now it's my turn to make a coffee for us,' she mentioned. With renewed confidence in her step, she went to the kitchen to do her duty. When Anna returned, she warned her new lover, 'dear Sam, the coffee's hot. So please be extra careful not to burn yourself.'

'I think it's a bit too late for that, don't you? As we've already been severely burnt,' he replied cheekily, and both burst into great peals of laughter.

'Also, be doubly careful about how you drink it, because maybe, my brooch could possibly be in your cup.' She then peered closely, saw nothing and laughed again. Suddenly, Anna jumped into his lap, triggering him to spill the coffee.

'Ouch, now look what you've made me do?' he said with annoyance.

'Never mind, darling,' she ignored her own careless actions in the haste of love. 'Do you know what?'

'What's that? I'm anxious to know,' he replied.

'Sam, you belong to me,' she outwardly declared.

'Ah, yes,' he quietly said, in a non-committal way.

'I love your moustache, it makes you look so manly,' Anna suggested, as she tugged it for a second time.

'Hey- stop it, ouch. Be gentle, woman, or do you not know the meaning of the word?' he reprimanded.

'What? Are you afraid that by the time I finish, you'll have no moustache left? So that being said, do you want some more?' she casually asked.

'More, more what?' he asked, as he needed some extra clarification about what she was referring to.

'I'm talking about coffee, Sam! What else did you think I meant?' she said while laughing hysterically.

'Anna, I think you're far hotter than any coffee a man could ever drink,' he mentioned. 'So, no, I'm fine for the moment.'

9

Anna let it be known she wished to visit Sam every day, so they could have a sinful time in bed together.

'Maybe one day a week would be safer…' Sam began to say, and then could go no further, due to uncertainty of how to further express his truth to her.

'My darling Sam, what do you mean, maybe one day a week?' she asked but before he could reply, she became once again, lost in her own thoughts as Sam breathed a sigh of relief. Perhaps one day, he would like to come and live in Plymouth. This made Anna feel exhilarated and only confirmed the belief that Sam indeed loved her.

9

The time finally came for Anna to return home, before school finished. She readied herself for departure from the property.

'My darling Sam, I have to go,' she clearly mentioned, feeling physically and emotionally satisfied in every way.

'Yes of course. Your family are waiting. And my parents could return home from working in the fields any minute. It would not work in our favour to get caught together like this,' he asserted.

'Okay, you're absolutely right. But when can I see you again?' she enquired.

'Hmm, maybe at a picnic, town, park or shop, where we can discuss things further next time we meet,' he replied.

'This is not answering my question, Sam. I want to know

exactly when and where we can next take our clothes off?' she seriously asked.

'Anna, I told you, don't rush me! There'll be plenty of opportunities before I have to leave,' Sam reassured her as he raised his voice.

Anna hurriedly kissed him, sat on the coach, and waved a fun-filled cheerio.

CHAPTER 7

Sam had initially came on vacation to visit his parents, but he'd unexpectedly fallen head first into a love affair. Something he never thought would ever happen to him! He quickly descended into a state of anxiety due to the unpredictable things had suddenly occurred. Attempting to dig himself out of this pickle, he tried to find some viable solutions as to how he and Anna could live a happy and peaceful life together.

He wondered what he should do now, seriously examining the situation with more determination. He had met two unique women of different ages and marital status. Anna was married and had a son. She was attractive, seductive and highly experienced in the art of making a man happy. On the other hand, Elena was a shy, non-pushy, beautiful, single, and sensible young girl. Judging from his meagre analysis of her, he leaned more towards Elena as the better option for him. Oh yes, she was more his type of woman, who would better suit Sam than what Anna ever could. How can a solution be found to this dilemma? Who should he favour? Or maybe, he could grab his belongings and disappear without a trace, which would put to rest any scandalous story about Anna that could break out.

And if this should happen, Sam had to consider how his poor parents would react. No, he wouldn't possibly do that, for their sake! Just imagine what they would say. *Oh, dear Lord, our son has run away to be with that floozy woman, Anna. Goodness, doesn't he love us anymore? Does he not care about what the people in the village are saying? Our prodigal son has become insane, on the verge of definite doom! In the name of the Father, Son and ...* Sam knew this would lead to disaster for his parents, and he could never do that to them.

'Why? Why has this happened? Please Lord, help me!' he howled aloud in desperation.

§

A few days passed without incident. At home, Anna is busy recapturing her love affair with Sam in her stormy mind. Meanwhile, Sam was well and truly caught in Anna's dubious claws, trying to outmanoeuvre his lust, and struggling to escape from the quicksand of love.

§

I can't live this way any longer, Anna thought, feeling frustrated one morning. She went directly to Sam for a second time, after completing her regular duties and dropping Adrian off to school. On this particular occasion, she was more frantic than ever to get to her lover and kept whipping the horses harder so they would break out into a full-blown run.

'Faster, you worthless horses! Since when do you know what it's like to desire something absolutely? Hurry up and be there,' she screamed, and they did. In no time at all, she arrived, all flustered and mentally on-edge.

As she stopped at the front yard, she wasted no time in jumping down from the coach, whip and bag in hand as she marched towards the door.

Sam noticed Anna approaching and thought to himself, *oh no, she has returned.* He hadn't expected her to come back so soon after the last time.

Suddenly the door opened widely. She burst inside, looked around and observed Sam standing there, watching her.

'Sam, are you alone?' Anna asked him, getting straight to the point.

He simply nodded his agreement.

'That's good to know,' she exclaimed, as she continued to approach him. 'Sam, I'm so sorry. I couldn't stay away any longer. I can't live without you.'

'What? Anna, stop it, don't be so silly,' he implored, stunned by her unusual and erratic behaviour.

'Stop what? On my arrival, you should run to hug and kiss me, as I'll be soon your darling wife. Shame on you!' she yelled at him.

He did as she demanded. Once Anna was happy again, he felt it was safe to continue. 'But Anna, please calm down. Think realistically about what you're saying. We can be lovers together for a short time, but you have to accept the fact that one day, we will be parted through necessity,' he reasoned quietly, trying to ignore the blood boiling in his veins.

'So, what are you trying to say?' she asked with suspiciously wary eyes.

'Anna, I have to say that I never expected for us to become so emotionally attached to each other so quickly,' he replied, with hesitation.

'You didn't? I did. Is there anything wrong with that?' Anna said, a distinct cold edge to her voice. She absentmindedly tapped her shoe with the whip.

'Anna, we need to have a long and serious talk about us, somewhere but definitely not here and not now please,' he begged.

Trying to change the subject abruptly, Anna blurted out on the spur of the moment, 'Sam, tell me something. Is she coming between us?'

'What's that? I don't understand the question? Anna, who are you talking about?' he answered, truly clueless as to what she was on about.

'It's simple really, my dear Sam. I'm talking about that other woman who was present at the picnic with us, on that most memorable day at the waterfall! You know exactly who I'm talking about. There's no point in denying it. You are lots of things, but you're certainly not stupid.'

'Oh Anna, this insane conversation is starting to get increasingly more difficult to comprehend,' he stuttered, knowing exactly what she had meant. He just wanted to buy himself more time.

'No, Sam, I think this is far easier than you think,' she said, pacing backwards and forwards the full length of the room a couple of times. She returned to Sam when she suddenly stopped and kissed him roughly. 'Hmm, my darling, tell me what's going to be in my coffee cup this time. No button, no brooch. Oh, tell me, what will it be?'

'Oh yes, indeed, I'll make us both a coffee!' he declared, breathing a sigh of relief that he could escape her clutches for a mere moment.

'Make it a plain one thanks, nothing fancy,' she ordered with suspicion.

'Just a plain one, coming right up,' he confirmed, and soon returned with two cups of steaming coffee.

Upon his arrival however, he saw she was even more hot tempered than before and Sam became alarmingly concerned about how to handle Anna. He preferred not to talk to her at all. Hoping she would get the message and leave him alone before his parents came from working in the field.

Sam began to contemplate all sorts of madness in his mind. *What if I told her never to come back? What would she say and do? If she complied, then all would be well for me but what if she didn't? What if she was persistent and decided to defy me by saying, 'You're an unworthy son of a bitch. Now I'll show you who I really am and how easy it is for me to destroy you if you dare say no to me. I'll ruin the dreams of your family as well. You rotten lecherous man! You only wanted me in your bed. Damn you to Hell. You deserve to drown in a sea of poison. All you should have is a plastic dummy to suck on, not my curvaceous body. How dare you? The first few days were fine, but now you start getting cold feet about us, because of that little tart, Elena. Whom do you really love? It's either me or her, you despicable male creature! Your pathetic lies and excuses will only make things far worse.*

From these horrible, uncontrolled, and unpredictable thoughts about the future what-if's, Sam's face suddenly turned a whiter shade of pale. He didn't even notice the time go by, so focused upon his own fears.

9

Meanwhile, Martin and his wife were heading home earlier than expected when they noticed the horses tied to a coach in front of their property.

'Look, Vivien. I think Peter Henderson has come to visit,' Martin assumed.

'Are you sure those are his horses?' his wife enquired.

'Yes, of course they are. Maybe he's not working on the ferry today, or it could be something else?' he commented, shrugging as the two made their way into the house.

At this precise moment, Sam had his hand on Anna's shoulder in an intimate way when his parents finally walked into the room. He swiftly lowered his hand in order not to raise any suspicion, but he was already too late.

'Oh sorry, please excuse us for coming in unannounced. We came home early from work. Mrs Henderson, it's so great to see you again. And may I enquire, where is your husband, Peter?' Martin asked, as he looked around.

Anna swallowed and cleared her dry throat, nearly being caught red-handed.

'Peter is carrying out his job at the ferry. I kind of arrived here by chance,' she lied, her cheeks beginning to blush.

'Well anyway, whatever is the case, it's always nice to see you,' Martin said, trying to put her at her ease.

'Oh, dear Anna, you look so lovely today,' Sam's mother politely mentioned.

Because of her recent dishonesty, she spoke of Sam's parents. Anna let out a single word which was 'brooch'. The word simply erupted out of control from her mouth. She had no power to stop it. Of course, she knew it made no sense to say such a thing, especially after his mother had kindly paid her a sincere compliment.

'What's that, dear?' Vivien asked, giving Anna a quizzical look.

'I'm sorry, I meant to say that I lost my brooch the last time I came to your home. So, I decided to come here looking for it instead,' she said without hesitation. Hoping she could cover her tracks as to why she was there without her husband.

'Oh no, this is very unfortunate. How could that have possibly happened? I've cleaned the house from top to bottom a few times since your last visit, but I found no unexplained brooches lying around, although I could be wrong. It has to be in the house somewhere,' she comforted Anna, who tried her best to look sad and distraught.

'Mother dear, don't worry about the brooch too much. I'm sure Anna will find it later down the track, in her own home,' Sam suddenly interrupted, side-stepping away from Anna and trying to kill any misunderstandings.

How would they react if they knew the real reason as to why Anna came here by herself? They would say, *'she's a married woman, for God's sake. How could you do such a wicked thing? Oh, you brought great shame and pain upon our family name. She's probably only doing it to satisfy herself, but you'll fall into a hole of rock bottom destruction. Elena was the right girl for you, but you deliberately blew it. If you would have chosen her instead, the world would have blessed you but now you'll be condemned by that same world!'* This thought echoed loudly, creating huge caverns where fear could freely crawl through the crevices of his mind.

If my parents were to know, they would surely tell Peter, and he would never let me be at peace again. He would create Hell on Earth- might throw me and my family out of the house, and I would then be to blame if my parents were left homeless, living on the streets. Peter could be quiet and relaxed, but in a situation such as this, he could unleash the monster within and could even possibly kill me! He could swiftly put a knife to my throat. Peter could easily threaten him and yell, you are nothing but a Casanova-type scoundrel. How dare you defile my wife? I trusted you. He could feel Peter's possible roaring words raging out of control. *When we meet, he now says hello my good friend, but if he found out about the ugly truth, he would then rightfully say, 'get out of here, you filthy dog.'*

The whole town of Plymouth would probably know about what happened then and laugh their nosey little heads off? What would become of Anna? Would Peter throw her out of his and Adrian's lives forever, or would he forgive and welcome her back? Assuming Adrian would have no clue about what events had just unfolded.

¶

Anna, while still on the property, used her communication skills as to not raise any possible mistrust about Sam and herself. She spoke sweet words, acted relaxed and smiled every now and again, as she would have done on any other visit. As if nothing untoward had ever happened.

'Oh, I'm starving. I'll go and make us some snacks. Would you like some coffee, dear?' Vivien sweetly enquired.

'Oh, no thank you. Maybe next time and please, do enjoy your meal.' She then looked at her watch and continued. 'Oh my! Look how the time has flown. I should be getting back home,' Anna smoothly replied.

'Well, if you say so Mrs Henderson but we'll keep looking for your brooch,' Vivien assured her.

'Oh, thank you,' Anna said as she nodded to Vivien. She took a quick scan at Sam, who stood there, shell-shocked. She then walked outside and rode away without a backward glance.

¶

For the rest of the day, Vivien found herself feeling quite restless, questioning the mysterious disappearance of Anna's brooch. Even at nightfall, when everyone was asleep, she could not get the pestering situation out of her mind and moved towards her husband to wake him.

'Martin, she's starting to worry me.'

'Betsy, is that you?' a semi-conscious Martin grumbled, partly dreaming and partly awake.

'No, no, I'm not her. It's me, Vivien, your wife.'

'Ah Vivien, what do you mean? Who is worrying you? Is it me you're concerned about?

'No, it's the brooch. It's giving me nightmares.'

'Are you crazy, woman? I don't care about your stupid jewellery. I just want to go back to sleep. Please leave me alone.'

'Martin, it's not my brooch I'm talking about. It belongs to Anna. I don't know where it could be. I swept the floor- moved all the furniture and cleaned everything, but I can't find it anywhere.'

'Look, we have a long and tedious day's work ahead of us tomorrow. So, please let me sleep in peace and you do the same as well. We can both worry about the damned brooch tomorrow.'

'I'm sorry, Martin. I just don't know how she could have lost it here.'

'I believe Anna was thinking about Sam when she said she lost her brooch.'

'What do you mean? Are you saying that Sam is a brooch?'

'No, but he is a brooch with two legs instead of a pin. Now go to sleep and stop pestering me,' replied an indignant Martin.

'Hmm, a brooch with two legs? Perhaps it walked out of the house after Anna then?' Vivien replied, before rolling over to shut her eyes.

❡

At her own home, Anna was feeling anxious about her affair with Sam. If someone were to see them together in a compromising position, then their relationship would be known to everyone. The only thing Anna knew for certain was she could never let this happen, at any cost!

She made brief contact with Sam and said, 'let's meet and go on a picnic somewhere near the river, away from prying eyes and listening ears.'

He agreed to her latest request.

¶

After a few days' time, Anna and Sam were lying in the grass, talking and laughing. Out of nowhere, Anna got up and threw water from the river at Sam. He was startled and before he could say anything, Anna explained.

'Sam, I think it's the right time that I baptise you to become my new husband. If only you could be me for a minute, then you'd truly know how much I love you,' she mentioned.

'Anna, I would try being you, but I'm not and if you were me…'

'I know what I would do. I would marry my sweet Anna. Sam, why do you fret so? We are the lucky ones. We came to know each other by sheer chance and we are now forever in love. My dear, we are joined by the heart and we are basically husband and wife now anyway. Isn't that true?'

'Yes, it is,' he said, but she was not yet satisfied with his answer.

'I'm waiting on your sincere answer, Sam, so tell me honestly, do you love me?'

'Anna, I … I truly love you,' he reluctantly replied.

'I knew you loved me. Now tell me, when are we going to get married? Sam, I want so much to be your lawfully wedded wife.'

He sighed and bit his lips. She doesn't know when to give up. 'Not now, Anna, I'm currently occupied in my studies. We will become husband and wife, only when the time is right.'

'I need to know when Sam, so I can divorce my husband.'

'*Divorce!* Why divorce?' he screeched.

'This is what the law requires. Both parties have to be single first in order to be married. If that's not the case with me, I would then be branded a bigamist and would then be promptly sent to jail.'

Hmm, he wasn't quite sure what to say but finally he found the words. 'We will surely be married, but as I said before, let's not rush it, Anna.'

'Sam, I can no longer live with my husband. He promised me everything, but instead, he has delivered absolutely nothing.'

¶

Anna was on the edge of insanity. She was so much in love with Sam that she was delving deeper and deeper into a dark tunnel, where leaving her child and murder were two possible options. Surely there were going to be dire consequences if she ever decides to her thoughts into play, but no one could know exactly what. Not even Anna herself knew.

If something were to happen to Adrian now- an unfortunate

death perhaps, then Anna would have chosen Sam over her own son. Or alternatively, could she tell Peter what she was about to do and how she wanted a divorce? She would say, *'Peter, you're no longer my husband. I don't love you anymore. Sam is the new man in my life now.'* How would Peter react? Would he simply say, *'that's not much of a surprise? I could see you liked him from the first day you met. Besides which, half of the world's population is female and one of those women will be mine too, even better looking than you. So, I say goodbye, good luck and good riddance to bad rubbish.'* This would be Anna's dream come true. It would give her the freedom she sought, to be with Sam.

❡

Anna and Sam were still relaxing on the grass, so she decided to probe him further about the matter of them being together.

'What are you going to get me as a celebratory present?' she asked with curiosity.

'I will give you everything in this world and more if you ask for it,' he replied.

'But not Peter, for he is yesterday's man, while you are my present and my future,' she whispered into his ear, and then promptly bit it without any warning whatsoever.

'Anna, would you stop that? First it was my moustache, then the hair on my chest and now my ear. What are you, a cannibal?' Sam replied in frustration.

'By the end of our affair, I will have eaten you whole,' she laughed merrily.

Sam did not bother joining in with the laughter. In fact, he inwardly cringed at such a gruesome idea.

¶

Later, at home, Anna went through her future plans in her mind. However, Sam was thinking about both Anna and Elena. They were like polar opposites of each other. One was like screechy old chalk, while the other was a tasty morsel of young, fresh, immature cheese.

Whenever he was around Anna, he couldn't do or say anything against her. He knew he was hopelessly tied around her little finger. When she said jump, he jumped. For that reason, he was weak and powerless and could not say no! Anna is smart and cool enough to manipulate him. When she is not around, he is a completely different person, where he sometimes even has hateful ideas about her.

In contrast, most of his thoughts about Elena are positive. She is a beautiful, warm, cute and clever girl. *And she is the one who should be waiting for me to ask her to be my girlfriend, not Anna.* In Elena's company, he could talk freely and express his feelings honestly. Anna on the other hand, kept on talking, but never really listened. She entertained him and made sure she was at the top of her own agenda, Sam right beside her. Anna was a woman with a fiery temper, who did not forgive easily. She wanted everything her own way, when she wanted it, and be damned to anyone who tried to stop her.

Sam finally made his decision: he must begin seeing Elena. He innately knew Anna was the wrong woman for him. She would bring him only complications, not peace.

He realised his mistake, and came to a frightening conclusion that Anna was on her own love adventure. Sam believed she loved Peter, but having met Sam, she'd transferred her love to him. But what happened if she tired of Sam a bit later? Would he be replaced by yet another man? Sam wanted someone to love him for who he truly was, not someone who used love as a bargaining tool to get what she wanted.

Who could he turn to for guidance on this matter? No one came to mind. He needed to sort it out for himself. Talking about it with Anna was like hitting his head up against a brick wall. Sam knew he had to defend himself against a future attack and somehow become a stronger person, but how? He told Anna he loved her, but did he really? Or was it something else? He could admit he lied and used Anna as a physical release, but anything more than that was simply not on the cards.

If he encouraged Anna, Sam would never again think about another woman, give his whole life to her, and marry her the next day. But this would not be the case with her: Sam convinced himself enough to know this fact. Anna began to fade from Sam's mind, but he was then rudely reminded that it was himself who gave her the initial idea in the first place, that Anna should leave her husband. That was not the right approach to adopt towards a viable solution. And heaven forbid if she did get divorced, Sam would then be well and truly committed, till death do they part.

Oh, Hell! What a mess. I will demand we split and end this affair now, before anyone gets too hurt, but how and when do I broach the matter? She won't easily forget all this! Anna is guaranteed to open her big mouth, and spread lies about me to anyone who would listen. All the time, plotting my demise and giving me the dreaded kiss of death when the time was ripe.

§

Day by day, Sam is feeling somewhat guilty by encouraging Anna, and found he could not sleep well at night. He would often arise to shake his head free of disappointing, vile thoughts. He lost his appetite and tried to read, but nothing was helping. *Jesus Christ, I'm in deep trouble. How will I be able to pass through this pain?* He wanted to run away from his demons, but how can he do that? Who could he confide in? People might say, 'what a wretched wasted space he is, running around after a married woman. What was he thinking?' Or they might suggest, 'leave that slut of a woman. She left her husband for you and will do the same again with someone else, and so it goes, on and on, it never stops.' And Sam believed the perception of these people would be spot on.

He kept tossing and turning in bed, trying to find ways to react to Anna's possible threats if he chose to end it all. With these thoughts firmly set in his mind, he experienced his first nightmare, in which she appeared and gave him an undeniably clear, simple message.

'My dear Sam, I see you're avoiding me, but remember, I am still carrying your baby.'

'What? What did you say? Oh, my Lord, Anna, you must be joking. We only did it the once.'

Anna continued talking. 'Sam, what we did was not a joke, it's your baby! Remember the time when you whispered in my ear- my sweet Anna, I will give you all of what I have and more, if I should only ask. Well, that was the moment I became the mother of your child.'

'No! No! Anna, you can't be pregnant. I'm still single, I'm still studying and it's extremely difficult for me to believe what you say is the truth.'

He suddenly woke from his nightmare and kept lying on the bed for a long time, with a sweat soaked sheet covering his head. Sometime during the night, he again once fell into sleep and the nightmare continued, for worse.

'Darling, I'm here again! Sam why do you worry so much? You are an agronomist, as your son will grow up to be one too. He will be proud to take after his daddy.'

'No, no, no!' he screamed out in agony before jumping out of bed. He tripped over the chair that was located nearby and fell hard, making a noise loud enough to wake the dead.

His mother clearly heard it, thinking a thief had broken into their house, so nudged Martin in the ribcage and loudly whispered, 'Wake up! I heard a strange thumping noise inside the house!'

'Hmm, what? What kind of brooch?' he grumbled.

'No brooch this time, we're being robbed,' an enormously scared Vivien exclaimed.

'Two, three… how many did you find?' he muttered, still in half asleep mode.

'Oh Martin, I'm frightened! It's the thief, the same one who took the gold brooch that Anna lost. In fact, he could be under our bed right now,' she complained.

'How many gold brooches do you have, woman? You're not making any sense whatsoever,' sleepy Martin asked. As he said this, he stood up with some grand difficulty and obediently looked under their marital bed. 'Nothing to report here, darling, except I did see some real smelly golden socks instead,' he replied.

Knowing his wife was still not satisfied; Martin then went into Sam's room and switched the light on.

'Oh, holy Hell. Thief, you're still here? Vivien, come here this instant. Your gold thief is stuck in our chair!' he commented.

'Martin, did you catch him?' she yelled with an equal mix of excitement and relief. She looked from a reasonable distance, just in case. She then noticed it was their son calmly sitting there.

'Open your god-damned eyes, Martin. It's only Sam,' she said, feeling safe once more and so fully entered the room.

'Vivien heard that you stole the golden brooch from under our bed, so hand it over, now.'

'Martin, you're hopeless. This is Sam, he's not a thief,' she hollered at her husband.

He stopped for a moment to rub his sleep filled eyes, getting a better look at who was really there. 'Ah yes, yes! You're right, my dear. So it is,' Martin replied, now fully alert to his surroundings and feeling highly embarrassed.

'Oh, thank you Lord, no more thief,' Vivien crossed herself and went back to their bedroom.

'Son, what's wrong? Why do you sit there and worry?' Martin asked, with a concerned and questioning look on his face.

'I just had an awful nightmare about someone,' he uttered while shaking his head.

'Hmm, me and your mother, we've been having nightmares about Anna's brooch. What was yours about?'

'It was so terrible, awful, and disastrous. I wouldn't wish such a dream to befall upon even my worst enemy,' Sam said.

'I understand about nightmares in people of your age, my son,' Martin mentioned and put his hand gently on his shoulder to offer support. Sam jumped from overstress, at his father's unexpected and caring touch.

'It's okay, I'm not your worst nightmare. It's all part of a normal process of maturing and becoming wiser in age. Just remember that to be single, you experience nightmares. To be a married man, you then have a mountain load of trouble which will suffocate you if you are not careful. So, go back to bed now. Tomorrow is another day. Good night, Sam, pleasant dreams,' Martin said and left his son to ponder the meaning of his words of advice, grabbing some extra sleep time for himself.

After his dad left the room, a still distressed Sam continued to dwell upon his unholy situation while lying in bed.

If I were to marry Elena, I know that cunningly swift and evil Anna would have my guts for garters and quickly condemn me. If this should happen, I would say, 'Anna, you're not my type of woman. *I won't marry you, so please just leave me alone and go away. I'm sorry, but you have no right to harass me anymore.'* The most difficult task was to find a way to be rid of her completely from his life. In a way that ensured she does not hurt anyone else important to him while staying happy herself. What an impossible task.

Well after midnight, with the curtain of sleep finally falling over his eyes, Sam entered into a dreamless state of being.

CHAPTER 8

For the past forty-eight hours, Sam behaved as if he had become somewhat lost and disorientated, because he kept thinking about Elena. He knew where she worked in Plymouth and decided to meet her the first opportunity he could get. *I have to see her,* he pondered, and on the very next day, went directly to her shop.

Elena was most surprised to see him there, as she never believed in her wildest dreams he would ever travel there to speak with her.

'Oh Sam, how great it is to see you again,' she said happily.

He was eager as well. 'Elena, I was passing by. Decided to drop in for a few minutes and ask how you've been since the last time we saw each other.'

A few customers also made an entrance at the same time as he spoke these words.

'Oh, excuse me for a moment, Sam- while I attend to these people,' she requested.

While she was busy looking after their needs, Sam looked around and spied a bunch of flowers in a vase sitting on the countertop. *They are very nice flowers,* he thought, and that is when she returned to speak with him again.

'Well Sam, as you can see, this is where I work.' She stated the obvious because of her nervousness.

'A very well organised shop you have here. I most definitely like it,' Sam praised.

'Why thank you, kind sir,' she said in a quiet but sweet voice.

'I see you're busy, with women coming in all the time. I don't want to disturb you, so what if I come back later when you're less preoccupied?' he asked.

'Oh no, Sam! You don't need to leave, you'll be alright. It's all okay, truly,' she quickly said. 'I can easily help them and talk to you as well. I'm quite capable of multitasking, you know.' With this, she went to attend to their millinery demands. On return, she said, 'well, I'm back, better late than never.'

'I've been noticing these beautiful flowers,' he said as he fondly touched them.

'Yes Sam, they are special. These are the same flowers we collected together on our first meeting. Do you remember?' she enquired.

'Oh yes, of course I do,' he agreed as he quickly revisited the recent past in his mind, careful not to say too much to avoid possible embarrassment on his part.

'They still have a lovely fragrance, although they're now diminishing, but are still alive. Besides which, I don't yet have the heart to throw them out,' Elena said.

'Yes, they are the flowers of …' He didn't finish the sentence.

'Yes Sam, they are the flowers of our …' she also stuttered.

Both had the word 'love' in mind, but hesitated to say it openly. Again, she left him to his own devices.

Oh, I'm so glad I've taken the time to come and visit, he thought while happily watching her communicate with her clientele.

She too was trying hard to catch glimpses of him from across the room and discreetly directed a barrage of smiles toward him. In some cases, she even made stupid errors while counting the money, but her friendly female purchasers would always correct her with kindness. They could clearly see her mind was on the only gentleman present in the store.

'Oh, please accept my sincerest apologies. It's my mistake,' she would say congenially to them.

Feeling Sam's presence at such close proximity, Elena was quite flushed. It felt like the most natural thing in the world for him to stand there. Sam was such an amazing man. Elena liked his attitude and in her young eyes, he was like a dashing hero, come to sweep her off her feet. Of course, she wanted to tell him all this, but etiquette held her back.

In Elena's presence, Sam felt her closeness, tenderness, and honesty. Anna, on the other hand, lacked all of these essential qualities.

Naturally, at Elena's young age, she was a bit nervous and confused, but this was a sign of her attraction towards men. Sam was captivated. Whilst standing near Anna, on the other hand, Sam reacted with entirely different feelings. When Anna opened the door, she immediately threw herself into his arms, demanding what she lacked and saying, '*oh Sam, I love you. I want you to be my husband. Do you understand?*'

Whereas Sam has only been with Elena a few times in different circumstances and each time, both felt a growing sense of mutual love, calmness, and respect towards each other.

As Sam went to stand, he tried to touch her shoulder, but she naturally moved away in reflex.

'Sam, please don't. Not yet,' Elena mentioned, timidly blinked at him.

While comparing the two women and thinking back to Anna, he was strongly reminded that she would have opened her mouth willingly for a kiss, while saying, *'yes… yes, my darling. I'm not shameful. Touch me… strip me naked and take me to your bed now.'*

Conversation was difficult in Elena's shop because of her job, and she left to once again be of service. Of course, she wanted to remain in his presence as much as she could, but restrained herself because of a natural shyness. On her return, Sam made another attempt to touch her. This time on the cheek and that, she allowed him to do.

'Elena, how can I say this…' Sam hesitated to continue, as he was beginning to feel a tad awkward with what he wanted to say next. 'Elena, you are such a pretty young woman.'

'Oh, Sam,' she exclaimed while looking into his eyes and inwardly thought, *just ask me for a kiss and I will respond.* But Elena kept quiet and waited.

'Do you realise that every minute I stand here, looking at you, dear Elena- you are becoming more and more transcendingly beautiful, and I can also see clearly you have a generous and loving heart.'

She lowered her head, blushing like a schoolgirl. She didn't know how to respond, but wished he would continue speaking his words of love. *Are you going to kiss me, Sam?*

He looked around to make sure nobody was watching, and stood directly in front of her. He gently lifted Elena's chin and looked straight into her blue eyes.

My darling, I know what you're thinking right now. Until now, nobody has ever kissed me and I'm wishing you'd be the first person to do that. Oh Sam, I can't refuse this strong desire I feel inside me, one which can be satisfied only by a dashingly handsome man like you. Sam please, how long do I have to wait for your warm, sweet kiss?

At last, they were alone in the shop. This is when his natural instincts kicked in and pushed him even closer to Elena. He could wait no longer. Sam lovingly kissed her on her warm, ruby red lips.

He is my one true love, she thought as magical energy embraced them and grew bigger to encompass the whole of the room. They stood there, enraptured with each other.

'I'm so sorry, Elena,' he profusely apologised and gently touched her flushed cheeks.

'Why? I enjoyed it,' she responded, knowing he was the one who had taken up residence in her beating heart. *He said I am a beautiful woman, but when is he going to say, 'I love you?'* In her mind, she could also imagine replying to him with those same words.

Pleasant pictures rushed through her preoccupied thoughts. She could clearly see herself with Sam in the church, kneeling at the altar, with Father Greene officiating. A gospel choir singing in the background, the exchange of rings, a wedding bouquet, softly lit candles burning. Herself wearing a long white dress with magnificent train and veil, with Sam as her husband.

Suddenly, Elena had second thoughts and remembered what she had brazenly said to Sam. No God-fearing, decent girl would ever say that, even if she did think it. Saying and doing belonged in two different worlds. So, she reluctantly pulled herself from the brink and said instead, 'no, Sam. We can't do this; not here, not now.'

Sam was not surprised and knew Anna would never have said no to him, but instead only ever said, *'yes, yes! Please Sam, yes.'*

He understood and accepted that Elena didn't want to look like a fool or ever be considered as a scarlet woman. She didn't want to be seen as being a despicable person in the eyes of the community, which she cared about and certainly didn't want false rumours circulating. They would judge harshly and say, *'she was such a sensible young girl, but look how she's changed for the worst.'*

Elena, being a cautious person who always made the right decision, became hesitant to continue this romantic interlude in the shop. At the correct time, she would tell Sam whether she was his or not.

'Elena, please quickly tell me, when can we see each other again?' he eagerly enquired. Before she had a chance to reply, a consumer entered and forced him to wait.

'Oh, please excuse me. Next time. I promise. Good luck, Sam, but I really do have to go now,' she quickly said.

On departure from the shop, Sam waved to Elena. The elderly lady, who interrupted their previous conversation, saw his gesture and thought the friendly wave had been directed at her. On the verge of fainting with ecstasy, she quickly corrected her composure, and chose the same stool Sam had been sitting on moments before.

Elena walked toward her with concern, and asked, 'excuse me, madam, are you alright?'

'Oh, I would happily die for the opportunity to touch the naked flesh of the young gentleman who just left,' she remarked. Soon realising the gesture was intended for Elena, she made an attempt to explain herself. 'Oh dear, I'm so sorry for what I just said. I simply took it for granted that he was waving to me. What a silly, old fool I am. Never mind, you can have him, and all the best to you. He's more your age than mine anyway.' She then quickly tried to change the subject by telling Elena of the real purpose of her visit. 'Well, I've come today to buy a new hat.'

'Yes, my lady. I've got many nice hats, especially for you,' Elena replied and went to have a look for something that would be appropriate for the woman's station in life.

CHAPTER 9

'Well, I haven't got any hay left for my poor horses!' Peter bellowed at lunch. 'So, I have to go and get it from someone who keeps it in stock. Last time, the hay from Mister Walker was not of the same high quality that I am used to, but have no other choice but to buy from him again,' fumed Peter.

For Anna, news about lack of food for the horses was the last thing she was concerned about. *That's his problem, not mine. I have enough of my own problems,* she pondered.

'Anna, I'm off now to see Mister Walker, so I can get what I need!' he repeated himself, but this time in a much louder voice and abruptly left his home, having received no response from his disinterested wife at all.

9

While on the road to the Walker's place, Peter remembered their tenants had what he needed. *What a great idea. Let's go see Martin!* And so began to turn the horses in the direction of his old property instead.

When he arrived, Peter quickly realised that neither Martin nor Sam were home. However, Vivien was.

'Oh hullo, dear lady. I'm sorry to unexpectedly visit like this,' he said, bowing in respect and humility.

'Oh, Mister Henderson, you are always welcome here,' she greeted him warmly with a smile and asked about his family.

'They are fine, thank you,' he politely answered. 'Anna is happy, and Adrian is still doing very well at school.'

'Oh, this is most certainly good news to hear,' she honestly exclaimed. 'Just a couple of days ago, I saw your wife. Oh, she looked so gorgeous, cheerful, fresh, and full of life.'

'Well, it is true, Mrs Vivien, that time can appear to be flying too fast, where several days ago can feel like as if it was only yesterday,' he said.

'I know what you're trying to say, Mister Henderson, but I'm not wrong. It was definitely a few days, and *not* a few weeks ago that I saw Anna. I remember it very well. Because, when Martin and I returned from the field, we saw them inside the parlour standing close to each other, Sam's hand resting upon her shoulder. They both jumped apart with surprise when they realised we were there, at which point our son removed his hand quickly and we thought this was a most odd reaction to our presence. Anyway, your wife quickly explained that she was there, looking for her lost brooch,' Vivien replied.

'She was here? Hmm, I didn't know that…' Peter wondered as a sudden memory occurred to him.

That's interesting. I've seen her brooch many times at home. Maybe Vivien misunderstood what Anna had been saying? He was also unable to comprehend any possible reason as to why his wife would come by herself to search for something without him. But as he was in a hurry, he didn't have time to delve into the details about such things.

He therefore executed his purpose for the visit. 'Mrs Vivien, I'm interested in buying some hay for my horses. So, please excuse me, I'm off to see your husband at the field and have a quick chat with him.'

She nodded her head and said nothing.

Peter then left, only to find Martin working in the middle of a most spectacular sunflower plantation.

'Oh Martin, I'm so impressed, standing here in this amazing field of gold. You should be proud of what you've done,' praised Peter.

'Hah! It's really all about having a good patch of healthy soil, rich manure and of course smart agronomic plans and instruction,' Martin pointed out. 'And to be honest with you, these beautiful views, smells, and golden colour make a man want to spend the rest of his life here rather than return home,' Martin concluded. Both men started an seamless conversation.

'Martin, the real reason for me being here, is because I've heard you've got some high-quality hay for sale. Is that correct?'

'Yes, of course I have. Are you interested in buying some?'

'Yes, for my hungry horses.'

'Well, my friend, we have to then leave this area and go to the dry field instead, which is closer to the homestead,'

Martin proposed and went to the appropriate section, where countless stacks of hay could be seen, littering the space. While they were arranging the bales on the coach, Martin realised his son had turned up.

'Ah that's good. Sam's arrived to say hello,' Martin happily said to Peter as he saw him fast approaching them.

'Oh Martin, don't ever let your son leave. He brought gold to your field. Isn't that right, Sam?' Peter jokingly enquired.

'Yes, that's correct,' Sam replied.

Sam was unusually quiet as he shook Peter's hand, and forced himself to smile. He appeared to be quite scared and agitated by Peter's unexpected presence. Because of his sudden bout of shyness, Peter looked more closely at his friend, thinking to himself that he most definitely now knew that something had happened between his wife and Sam. Especially after remembering what Vivien had just told him some half an hour before, when he first arrived.

Sam hoped with all his heart that Peter did not know Anna had come here by herself a few days ago. Otherwise, a lot of questions on Peter's part would be asked. *Or perhaps, oh dear Lord, he already knows everything about us, but waited for the right opportunity to express it. Then with great angry thoughts, Peter will seek to punish me.* Sam felt a sudden chill rush up and down his spine. This time, Sam did not ask Peter how his family was as he would normally.

After loading the hay bales on to the coach, all three men stood under the shade to cool off. Martin, who was oblivious to his son's unfriendly and uncomfortable behaviour towards their visitor, went inside the house briefly and brought out some whisky and glasses.

'Ah, Mister Henderson, can I offer you a drink. Surely just one couldn't hurt, before you leave.' Before giving Peter a chance to say no, Martin quickly filled the glasses– one for himself and gave the other to Peter, in a gesture of friendship. 'And what about you, son?'

Martin offered, but Sam refused to partake. After some tall tales and stimulating conversation, Peter was ready to depart.

'Till next time,' Peter said, then shook hands with both men and went back home with the horse feed he had originally come for, but left with so much more.

Vivien ran from the kitchen in a mad dash, breathless. 'Where is Peter? Is he still here?'

'My dear Vivien, again you've come too late. He's already on the road,' Martin mentioned, embraced her and went inside.

g

Further along the track, Peter became restless thinking about Anna and her 'lost' brooch! I don't know when she lost it, but I saw that same piece of jewellery, every time I was at home. As she only has one brooch.

When Adrian was asleep later that night, Peter took the opportunity to ask Anna about her surprise visit to their rented property a few days ago, without him.

'Anna, I found a different man who had some hay today, so I bought some,' Peter began.

'Did you, dear? That's good. Probably this time, Mister Walker possessed better quality food than last time?' she said, still uninterested.

'No, not him! I'm talking about our tenant, Martin.'

'Oh Peter, you were at his place?' Anna enquired with an impending sense of doom.

'Yes, I was. Whilst there, Martin and I got into quite a most interesting conversation,' Peter said, with curiosity building within.

'Oh really, how are they?'

She nearly asked how Sam was, but restrained herself. She knew it would be a disastrous mistake if she did, so remained silent, which was most unusual for her.

'Before meeting Martin in the field, I also briefly talked with Vivien, and of course, you came up in the topic of conversation. She mentioned you were there a few days ago, looking for your lost brooch.'

'A brooch… What do you mean, a brooch?' she exclaimed with ignorance, sure to hide her lying face.

'Yes, she mentioned you lost it at their place last time we visited together as a family and how you returned to look for it all by yourself. Is that correct?'

Anna felt suddenly caught off guard. 'But, my dear Peter, I couldn't find it at home. I believed that I must have lost it somewhere and thought I'd find it at their place,' she squealed.

Peter didn't miss the note of fear he heard in her raised and shrilled voice. 'Anna, even after the time you're talking about, I always noticed the brooch still sitting in the place where you usually keep it. I don't understand.' Looking into her eyes, he sought to discover the real truth.

'My dear Peter, but that's impossible,' she stated unconvincingly and fought to control her anguished, foggy mind. *Perhaps Peter already knew about me and Sam, and this is why he is asking so many questions now. I have to be careful with what I say.*

Peter still harboured very real doubts in his mind, which was reflected in what he said next. 'How come you didn't let me know you were going to the property, or that you had even been there at all?'

'Peter, by the time you come home, it's late. We rarely have time to talk with each other anymore and without malice, I sometimes simply forget to tell you a few things.'

She stood there, looking miserably pale, knowing it was only a matter of time before Peter would come to know what was going on behind his back while he was working.

'Before I call it a night, there is just one more thing, if you could be so kind as to humour me with your answer. On the day they saw you unexpectedly, Vivien mentioned to me that as they walked in, they noticed you and Sam together in the parlour. That he was touching your shoulder in a gentle, most intimate way. Is this correct?'

These words ran like a sharp knife over her frozen, fearful heart.

'Well, Peter, for a start... we understood that his parents were already inside the house and nothing untoward- I can assure you, was going on between us. It was simply a friendly gesture that meant absolutely nothing to the two of us.' Anna herself was not sure that what she'd just said truly sounded believable to her husband's ears.

'Anna, why are you lying to me?' he exclaimed, in an angry and possessive voice. 'So, this is what you do when I'm working. You keep me in the dark as to your real whereabouts. This fact comes as a great shock to me. So, tell me, is all that I've been told today the truth?' he questioned her in a harsher tone than ever before.

'What are you talking about?' she asked awkwardly.

'Anna please, you know very well *who* I'm talking about! What a shame! The whole of Plymouth knows us as a well-respected family and now this scandal!' Peter then angrily slammed his fist hard on the table. 'People will spit and laugh at us! I can't afford that to happen, do you understand? Just think about what you're doing. Our son needs our love, support, and quality time from both of us. Are you going to overlook all these responsibilities, just to satisfy your own selfish needs?'

Peter's bitter words hit her with a thunderous force, striking fear into her heart and soul. Anna lowered her head in shame, about to burst into tears. *Why did I not think before I acted? How can I quickly get myself out of this mess? How will Peter react from now on?* Her only option was to wait and see, now that everything was out in the open.

¶

Peter was in a dilemma, for he was not sure if what he heard was the whole story! He considered the possibility it might be just an innocent misunderstanding, as Anna had said. *Something is happening with my wife but I'm not sure what exactly? Perhaps if Sam had never come to visit, nothing would have eventuated.* And in all the time he confronted her, she neither stood there with remorse nor apologised for deluding herself.

¶

On the morning after their altercation, and without bidding farewell to Anna, Peter went to the ferry to begin his day. The argument was still foremost in the front of his mind and did not leave him for a moment. This began to reflect in bad behaviour towards his innocent and non-involved passengers.

One of them laughingly remarked, 'hey there, Mister Henderson, did you get out of the wrong side of the bed this morning?'

'And what business is it of yours, sir, if I did or I didn't?' Peter grumpily replied.

'Psst, our Peter must be dealing with something difficult. Why is he so angry today? He has a charming wife, who is most faithful to him, with young Adrian as their greatest reward. We greatly respect them for being such a wonderful family,' another man piped up, defending Peter's out of character behaviour.

Peter so much wanted to blurt out the real situation, which left a bitter taste in his mouth. Because his first priority was to stop any nasty rumours and gossip from spreading about his family, he held back from spilling his guts to people who really should not know his personal business. Although, he still wanted to shout at his commuters and proclaim his so-called wonderful, respectful, and faithful Anna had been caught cheating on him.

At home, his son Adrian might ask, '*do I have another daddy*'? And in his innocence, he would plead with Peter by saying, '*let Mummy play with her friends in the same way that I do at school. She's a great mum. She drops me off without complaint, wishes me well each day, and then gives me a kiss goodbye. I love her very much and I know she loves me too.*' Peter's head started to spin with all sorts of dreadful imaginings. *Oh Lord, tell me- why did you create the human heart which absorbs all manner of sorrow, pain, worry, and other untold maladies?*

9

Anna found herself at a most difficult crossroads of her married life, all surrounded with signs: where do I run to, and to whom? Which way do I turn?

Completely shattered because of the fight which broke out unexpectedly between herself and her husband, Anna's mind kept circling this same point, again and again. All she wanted to do was run away from everything and everyone, including herself. She was left without vision for her future and lost all sense of identity. Strong emotions of great anger towards Sam came to the surface of her mind. As well as other altercations she had with herself, that when combined, made her blood boil over, filling her only with revenge.

Anna swore she would let Sam know what damage he had caused to the relationship between Peter and herself. Anna reasoned that it was all entirely Sam's fault, because he'd told Anna he would marry her. She was a fool to believe his words but still, her rejected, aching heart could not bear to let him go. Sam's promises, whether they be genuine or false, were a forever strong presence in Anna's soul. Far stronger than any cold, hard-steel cables that held Peter's stupid, boring, old ferry in place. Perhaps one day, it would sink.

9

She told herself, *I swear I need to be with Sam once more, to know for certain he loves me. He may say, 'Anna, we should not see each other anymore.' I feel he's trying to avoid me by making excuses. Am I so ugly, hunch-backed, blind, dirty, stinky, or crippled? Oh, I know who he's doing this for- that young so-called virgin still in her dawn, who is completely inexperienced and knows nothing about satisfying a real man. Yet, I think she has somehow managed to tear him away from me.*

She then remembered that once, a long time ago, her idiot of a husband said, 'Anna, go and buy yourself a new hat, to make you look prettier than what you already are.'

And this is exactly what she now intended to do. She will buy herself a spectacular hat and then later visit Sam. *He can't throw me out just like that, as I hold his balls in the palm of my hand! I will demand an answer from him: yes or no.* She might even mention Sam's baby, which was taking shape inside her womb. Full of her creative plans, imaginations, and delusions, she wasted no time in visiting Elena's shop.

Peter's sister was shocked to see her as Anna had never been there before.

'Hello Anna,' she exclaimed in wonder while greeting her sister-in-law. 'It's so wonderful you came to see me.'

'Oh well, my dear, times have changed, and you are quite right. I have come to see you,' she agreed with a smile.

'Oh, my dear Anna, tell me what news have you brought with you?' Elena asked politely, whilst regarding said reason as being quite strange and unusual.

'Well, I came to see what new hats you have for me.'

'Anna, there are plenty of choices to accommodate your personal style for everyday wear, special occasions. or simply for whimsical reasons. It really depends upon the circumstances. Personally, I believe new hats tend to be more attractive than older ones,' Elena informed Anna.

'Well my dear, I'm interested in buying only the best in your shop, so may I take a look around?' Anna asked.

'By all means, please do,' Elena said with courtesy, and left Anna to carry out her search.

While she was wandering through the shop, Elena observed her from a distance, and could clearly see that Anna was acting really odd, which caused Elena to become even more suspicious of why she was really there.

'Anna, you look a bit worried and quite exhausted. Are you okay?' Elena asked with a mixture of curiosity and concern.

'Ah dear Elena, life can be tough, or it can be easy. We are all but mere sufferers of time,' she cryptically remarked. Eventually she came across a hat which suited her needs perfectly. 'Oh yes, this is the one that's the nicest of them all.'

She proceeded to place it on top of her head and assessed her reflection in the mirror. 'Hmm, what do you think?' she asked, prompting Elena a response.

'It's absolutely charming. It suits you well and I'm more than sure you've made the right choice,' Elena replied, confirming what Anna already knew.

'Thank you. Thank you very much,' Anna said, as she continued to unashamedly survey herself in the mirror. 'Elena, please tell me, who is that woman in the mirror?'

She was keen to know Elena's response to such an unusual question.

'Well, that's easy to answer. Of course, it's no other than the elegant and well-respected Lady Anna Henderson.'

'Hmm, yes, you're absolutely right. It is truly me!' she whispered. 'Tell me now, how do I look?'

'Oh, but I have already said you look absolutely charming, but you also look new, young, and most attractive.' Elena spoke the words that Anna wished to hear, though it was in order to get the sale.

'New... you said new.' Anna was most happy with her response. 'Oh, my dear Elena, if I look new, then this must mean there is new hope too.'

What a strange thing to have said, Anna felt quite baffled by the real meaning of what Anna was trying to convey when she said 'new hope,' but chose not to ask any questions at this stage.

'Well, I've decided to buy this one and will try to start a new life with him,' Anna mentioned.

'Oh yes, you are absolutely right.'

Elena was under the assumption Anna was buying this hat to keep the relationship between her and Peter alive. In reality, Anna was thinking about different ways in which to impress Sam. Anna said goodbye to Elena, and hurriedly left the shop in a buoyant mood.

On the way back to her place of abode, Anna was strongly thinking about how not to lose Peter, whilst simultaneously keeping Sam. She wanted them both and was attempting to play Russian roulette with her husband and lover. In her mind, like a cunning old fox, Anna was already imagining the conversation she would have with Peter on her return home. '*My darling husband, I finally bought the hat which you once told me to buy. Do you remember suggesting that to me a long time ago?*' Anna believed the hat was a symbol with which their love could be rekindled. '*Peter, do you still love me? Please tell me, am I more attractive to you, now that I own this most charming hat. Oh please, let me feel the warmth of your kiss upon my waiting lips. And with renewed hope, I'll promise to make endless love with you, just to keep you happy and satisfied.*'

Upon arrival, Anna took the first opportunity to approach Peter and try out her new plan to entice him to stay with her.

'Peter, my dear husband, I want to tell you something.'

'Yes, what is it and if you should tell me, will I know what you're talking about?' he said.

'It's simple really. I bought a new hat today, as you suggested I should do quite a long time ago.'

'A hat, so what?' he replied, in a harsh and no-nonsense tone. 'If you bought it, then you're the one who'll be wearing it, not me.'

'But … but Peter, doesn't this mean anything to you?' she desperately asked.

He remained silent.

Anna, feeling petulant by this stage thought, if you're not going to admire the hat, then someone else will; someone like Sam. She took some deep breaths, to keep herself outwardly calm. There was no way on God's Earth she was going to give her husband the pleasure of seeing her so upset, at his uninterested responses. Although it was quite okay for Anna to play the same game of disinterest with her husband, when it suited her.

CHAPTER 10

One day, Adrian went to his mother to have a talk about what was on his mind. 'Mum, when will Mister Sam come to pay us a visit?' he keenly enquired.

'Oh Adrian, I don't know when he'll come to see us here. I guess it all depends upon him. Why do you ask?' she said.

'I like him a lot. I'm interested about his school and what he's learning. Mum, he must have lots of soil and seeds on his writing desk. Does he?' he asked with interest.

She felt quite perplexed at this last question that she could not answer. Instead, Anna simply said, 'Adrian please, that is his business, not ours. Maybe we will go back one day to his house to see him instead.'

'Mum, do you know when he'll go back to his dirty school?' he persistently continued.

'I don't know, honey. We shall ask Sam, when we next see him as to when he's due to leave and go back to his own studies,' she suggested and thankfully, her son dropped the whole subject.

The next morning, as Peter left for work, Anna got dressed and put lots of makeup and perfume on, in hopes of seeing Sam once again. With purpose in mind, she lovingly placed her new hat upon her head, stood in front of the mirror, smiled and she so badly wanted him to admire her sexy new look.

After eagerly dropping Adrian off at school, she embarked upon her real mission.

Her stormy speculations, combined with the thundering hooves of galloping horses, forced Anna to inwardly crumble, falling towards unstoppable disaster. Wrapped securely in this curtain of revenge and anger, she was now totally unpredictable. In her foggy mind, only one thing was clear at this stage and that was *him*!

When I see Sam, I'll ask him a simple question: 'why are you ignoring and abandoning me?' If I should receive a wrong answer, then I will demand his undying love and commitment to me forever.

Breathless, confused, and dusty, Anna was once again caught in the crossfire of her own tempestuous thoughts. A part of her was filled with lust and love for Sam, but there was also the other extreme. Where she wanted revenge on him for ruining her life. She wanted to lash out and hurt him, as he did to her.

Before she knew it, the journey came to an abrupt halt, outside of Martin's house. She was totally unaware of how she even got there.

Jumping off the carriage, she pondered for a moment as to her next move and finally decided to enter the house. While she was stood near the closed door, she corrected her hat, wet her lips, and wiped any excess dust from her chest and shoulders.

She bravely knocked, waiting for a response. When none came, she simply invited herself inside.

A moment after Anna's uninvited entrance, Lady Vivien appeared around the corner, surprised to see Peter's wife standing inside their house. It also seemed the hostess was in no fit state to greet anyone. Anna quickly observed that Vivien's hair was most untidy, with comb still held in her hand. She was also wearing a kitchen apron.

'Oh Lord, so very nice of you, Lady Henderson, to come and visit us again,' she said.

Anna simply smiled and bided her time.

'Oh, please excuse how shabbily I look, my dear lady,' Vivien apologised to Anna. 'As you can see, I look as if I'm a scarecrow just come in from the harvest field.'

Anna detected hints of discomposure in speech and behaviour.

'On the other hand, you're looking so pretty. But me, oh no,' Vivien emphasised.

'It's okay, you're fine. Everything is just fine,' Anna quietly mentioned, trying to put her hostess at ease. While battling to control herself from the anger she so strongly felt within.

'Please, make yourself at home.'

Anna gladly accepted the request.

'Lady Henderson, tell me how is your husband and cute little Adrian?' Vivien asked with interest.

'Well ... yes they are fine, thank you,' she answered briefly, consciously searching for Sam's whereabouts.

'Oh my, I see you're wearing a beautiful new hat. I like it a lot.

You must be so proud,' Vivien complimented her, thinking Anna was being unusually quiet. 'Of course, on a sophisticated lady such as yourself, any hat would look wonderful,' Vivien enthusiastically continued. 'As we all know, you have a mighty fine husband, who worries, looks after, and respects you, because he loves you. That's what makes you proud of him and him of you. Oh, my dear lady, to have such a husband is rare to find, among many.'

Sitting quietly without responding, Anna felt strangely uplifted by Vivien's words, which had a healing effect on her shattered heart. Still, her mind wanted to dwell in other dark places. Like where was Sam?

Vivien wrongly concluded the reason for Anna's abstinence from conversation may have been linked to the fact of her lost brooch. 'Oh, Lady Henderson, believe me when I say we've looked everywhere around the house for your brooch and couldn't find it anywhere. We were wondering whether you mistakenly misplaced it at your own home.'

In her absentmindedness, Anna disregarded Vivien's remark and posed a question to her instead. 'And please pray tell me, dear Mrs Vivien, what unpleasant things have happened to you, during your search?'

'Oh, dear Lord, I've spent many a sleepless night thinking, worrying and keeping a look out for your missing brooch, and we still haven't found it,' she responded.

'A brooch... what brooch? Whose brooch?' Anna's asked with surprise.

'Yours of course, my lady,' Vivien emphasised with a sad expression.

'Oh… yes, yes.' Anna suddenly remembered. 'Oh well, Mrs Vivien, don't worry about it, she is not…' she paused and rethought her statement, 'I mean, I got a new one,' she replied while touching her chest.

'Oh look, how nice!' Vivien's use of rhetoric perfectly accompanied her exaggerated tone. 'You are indeed a lucky woman, where your husband buys you everything you want. My Martin would never buy me such frivolities. He always said I was too old for that sort of thing, even when I was young. And what can I do but to comply with his wishes.' Her pale expression accompanied by the associated emotions would have affected anyone with a heart.

However, Anna remained adamant on finding Sam, ignoring Vivien's complaint. Having waited long enough, Anna nervously touched upon the subject of her son. 'Mrs Vivien, are you alone?'

'Yes, I am. Martin is in the field at the moment working and Sam will arrive in a short while. When you came, I was busy cooking dinner for them,' Vivien replied.

'Oh, I see. So, you mean Sam is not at home?' Anna quietly sought clarification and sighed.

'That's right dear. He's in town, shopping for some supplies,' Vivien mentioned. 'As you may know, it will not be long before he returns to university to continue his study. It would be great if you could visit before he leaves, to bid him farewell, Mrs Henderson. I'm sure he would appreciate this gesture on your behalf. Would you do that?'

'Hmm, I probably will,' Anna mentioned with a growing

anger and unease. She was also not in any generous mood to sit and listen to Vivien prattle on about nothing. *Ah, typical peasant chatter-box, she is. I'm not interested in her boring rubbish.*

Damn, where can I find him, Anna seriously contemplated. *He could be anywhere– walking the streets, drinking in the tavern, relaxing in the park, church…*

Then a sudden realisation hit her. *Oh yes, he is most probably at Elena's place of work.* She thought there was something fishy going on there. It was difficult for Anna to think straight with her mind was so clouded by her misjudgement. The mere fact he could be anywhere in the town, to the point that she didn't know where to start looking, was a major distraction. Anna considered the option of running into Elena's shop and breathlessly asking her where Sam was, but that would not be a smart thing to do. Anna was in no position where she could say anything to Peter's sister, but could easily imagine Elena's response instead. '*Hey, you're an idiot. You're a married woman and yet here you are, blindly running after a young single man, only to satisfy your own uncontrollable and lustful urges. You're despicable and besides which, what would I tell Peter?*'

Anna was willing to break all the rules to be with Sam one more time, and started preparing herself for Elena's responses. Anna believed that when the time came, she could easily manipulate Elena into telling her what she needed to know.

Without realising Anna was no longer listening, Vivien kept talking. She kindly offered her guest a drink and tried to maintain a friendly environment in which Anna could relax.

'Oh, my dear Lady Henderson, do look after yourself and Peter. Please, love your husband. Live for him and he will buy you heaps of beautiful hats, jewellery, shoes, dresses and more.' She then lowered her voice, in a conspiratorial tone and continued. 'Confidentially and just between you and me, if you don't love him anymore, he could change and become totally different. Yes, my dear, he could become like that man in town who bashed his wife so hard, her body was covered in bruises, black and blue. She couldn't talk and walk for months and was barely alive! And to make matters worse, while outside their home, he tore the clothes off her back, left her cowering naked on their doorstep, kicked her like a dog and then hollered, "vagabond, damn you to Hell! Get away from here and never come back." You see, my lady, this was because the woman's husband had just found out about her love affair with another man through idle chatter and town gossip. What do you think of such an awful scandal?'

'Interesting!' she replied. 'Well Mrs Vivien, I have to go now. I'll come again when I next get a chance.'

'With Lord's blessings, please do anytime,' she said. As Anna approached the coach outside, Vivien continued. 'And all the best of luck to you, dear lady, and please look after your brooch and that beautiful hat you are so finely wearing,' she reminded, and sent Anna off with a friendly wave.

Anna, on the other hand, while out of Vivien's earshot, was not so charitable and whispered under her breath, 'piss off, you unpleasant peasant!'

A few minutes into her journey, Anna experienced great

suffering, anger and revenge. They increased her determination and resolve to reach Sam, while feverishly continuing to create a mental picture about her competition. *Peter's sister was such a malignant creature, really. She would surely know where Sam was. After all, Elena has already got inside his head, where he now lusts after her. Evil virgin bitch. I hate her.* This caused Anna to furiously whip the horses with no mercy.

'Go faster, you dumb animals,' she yelled out loud. The poor horses were running at the speed of launched arrows. but still, she kept whipping them while continuing her verbal tirade. 'Sam, where are you? I demand to have you with me now!' she screamed into the wind with all her might.

In the wild surrounded with thick clouds of dust, Anna was completely out of her head! Ravaged with rage and vengeance, she threw herself into unthinkable circumstances which could have been avoided. She looked shocked, sweaty, and pale. She was breathless, her hat was hanging on her head by the slightest of strands. She was entirely covered with dust and as a consequence, hardly knew what she was doing.

When she arrived in town, she realised she had approached Elena's shop and stopped the carriage. Puffing with accumulated dirt, a tilted loose hat and whip in hand, she marched towards her destination, as a soldier marching off into battle.

Near the entrance, Anna twisted the whip until it nearly broke, before walking in. There were no customers, which was a good thing really for her.

At first, Elena didn't recognise the person who had entered, but soon was able to distinguish who it was through all the caked-on dirt and grime.

'Anna, is that you? Oh no, what's happened? Are you okay?' she quickly asked, but harboured different underlying thoughts. *Oh, dear Lord, there must be something badly wrong with her,* looking at her dishevelled appearance. If Elena was feeling any discomfort about this unpredictable situation, she determined not to show it.

Anna stood stationary, apparently oblivious to all external stimuli.

Elena tried to comfort her and said, 'oh my, I can see you're tired and run down- maybe you're feeling unwell. Please tell me, what's going on?'

'*Him!*' Anna said whilst continuing to breathe deeply.

'Anna please, I don't understand? What do you mean when you say 'him'? Do you mean Peter?' Elena responded and spotted the splotchy red eyes.

'No, not Peter, I'm talking about Sam,' Anna loudly exclaimed whilst correcting her appearance.

'I don't understand? What about him?'

¶

This is when Elena fully realised the depth of desire Anna had for Sam. *Oh Lord, she's crazy,* but later chose to turn this information to her advantage. *This is going to be interesting.*

'Anna, please sit, relax and then we can talk. Does that sound like a good idea to you?'

Anna didn't listen to Elena's words and chose to pace around the shop instead for a few more minutes, slowly gathering her composure. In doing so, she started to develop a believable story of what happened, which led Anna to experience a great sense of comfort.

'Oh yes, of course Elena, I'm sorry. My trip was very rough- I lost my concentration and somehow the horses brought me to your shop. They were galloping so erratically, to the extent that I believed I would lose my life! Oh Lord, it was such an awful experience. If Sam had been there, he could have held the horses back, and this whole horrible frightening trip could then have been avoided. I see him as a truly sturdy and dependable man. Do you know what I mean?' she asked.

Elena began to feel somewhat uneasy, and tried to reason away what had been said about the mix up of names. Heavy thoughts invaded her mind. Realising that nobody wanted to go through such a hair-raising event, Elena quietly replied, 'yes Anna, you are correct.'

'Oops, I'm sorry, Elena. I realised I've just made a mistake. At that moment when it happened, I was thinking about Peter, but while relaying my story to you just then… I mentioned Sam instead. I also must apologise for raising my voice. You don't deserve that from me,' Anna said tenderly and continued to try and cover her tracks. 'And yes, I was planning to come here with Peter, but he was busy on the ferry,' she continued, blatantly lying to Elena.

'Oh dear, what a pity he couldn't come,' Peter's sister mentioned without the slightest hint of sarcasm in her voice.

Though her personal opinions were completely riddled with it. 'But anyway, my dear, it's more important to know you are alright and recovering from your ordeal. With that being said, while you're here, would you like to buy another hat, like last time? Because the one you're wearing now is a bit worse for wear. Besides which, it will make you feel better,' she insisted, forever the smart salesperson.

'Yes, dear Elena. By all means, yes. Since I'm here, I might as well,' she willingly agreed.

Elena thought, *I know the real reason why you are here, dear sister-in-law. You want Sam and definitely not the hat. You were hoping to see him, weren't you? And that is why you rushed, like a bat out of Hell to get here.*

For a while, Anna fixed herself up, wiped off the remaining dust from her body and searched for a favourable hat. Thankfully, she quickly found a suitable one which would suit her nefarious purposes.

'Oh yes, this red one is most attractive indeed. I would even go so far as to say that men find red a most attractive colour more than others. Would you agree?' Anna asked.

'Well … yes,' Elena confirmed resentfully, knowing full well what Anna was really implying.

At the same instant, a woman entered the shop. Elena excused herself from Anna and went to serve the customer.

Anna stood in front of the mirror, looking at herself while trying on the hat, reapplying her makeup and muttering something under her breath.

She had the figure and personality which everyone

respected and admired. In people's eyes, she was a cool, relaxed, proud and charming lady with exceptional manners. Lurking within however, Anna was a total contradiction, where anger, jealousy, hatred and lust reigned supreme, shaping her thoughts into a squalid quagmire of toxicity.

While catering to her appearance, she kept thinking about Sam and the stupid bitch, Elena. *'Where can I find Sam,'* she wanted to blurt out. *Elena is still a virgin. She might not even know what real sex is all about? Should I ask if she has slept with anyone before, perhaps even with Sam? Maybe she is carrying his baby. Oh, what then? I wish I knew the answers to all these questions.* Anna herself imagined different possibilities and once again, began to feel uneasy with these ideas. Suddenly, she came up with a plan and decided to wait and see if Sam comes to the shop, *but how long will I have to wait?* She was still deep in reflection when Elena returned.

'Oh Anna, I just remembered. Sam did drop in here last week and told me how he would soon be returning to university. Maybe he'll never come back again! Are you sorry to know this?' she asked, wanting to know Anna's real feelings about that possibility.

'Well, how can I say this …' she stretched out her words slowly. 'You have a priority, you are young and single. You also have a whole lifetime in front of you,' Anna cajoled, though in her mind thinking Elena was simply idiotic. 'Oh, dear me, time is flying, I have to go,' Anna promptly said, and bought the red hat before madly rushing out the door.

Having left at such a frantic pace, and once on board the

moving carriage again, she spied from a distance, a young man walking on the other side of the street. It looked as though he was headed straight for Glory Hats. She immediately stopped the horses mid-stride and squinted. Yes, her intuition was correct. It was Sam, and it looked as if he was carrying something.

'Oh Sam, is that really you?' she asked herself and instantly felt as though boiling water had just been poured on to every part of her alert, itching skin. Watching Sam enter Elena's shop was something she could not bear to witness.

Thoughts now furiously bubbled inside her, many discordant elements were thrown into the cauldron of her brain. Anna wanted badly to jump off the coach and run to him, but managed to halt this strong desire from being converted into action. In a fiery ball of fury and insanity, more negative conjourings were concocted about Sam and Elena.

Damn despicable man. He went to her and not me. Anna twisted the whip to breaking point as she imagined what she wanted to say to him. *Oh yes, I will grab the chance to teach him a lesson he will never forget. He promised I will be his wife, but instead, here he is! Crawling on his hands and knees, to that ugly duckling instead. Hah. Who is the real liar to me- him or her? Damn them both to Hell. Because of Sam and Elena, my Peter has started hating me. They ruined my life. I will have to up my game. I will go and tell Elena what he once promised and how he made me pregnant! Yes, Elena will freak out of her tiny puritan mind upon hearing this piece of surprising news, and so drown in the river, to spare herself from having to deal with the scandal of Anna having an illegitimate child with Sam- the same man Elena chose to give her own*

heart to. Yes, Elena deserves to die. It's simple, he belongs to me, not her.
Enraged, Anna managed a laugh while waiting for Sam to leave.

While in this terrible state of limbo, just waiting, she suddenly heard an old woman say, 'hello Mrs Henderson.'

In Anna's shattered internal intensity, she was unable to hear her name being called.

'Mrs Henderson,' the elderly woman repeated, snapping Anna back to the present time.

Anna turned quickly around and saw who was speaking. 'Oh, Granny May, is that you?' she said with awe. 'Oh, I'm so sorry, I didn't hear you. Please forgive me for not answering immediately. I was a million miles away.'

'Mrs Henderson, can you please do me a huge favour?' the elderly lady asked with a rough voice.

'Yeah sure, Granny, I'm listening. Tell me, what is it?' Anna politely asked her.

'My home is too far from here. I'm old, my legs are tired, and my bag is too heavy. I don't know how I'll get home in this condition. Could you please give me a lift?' she begged Anna with a bad hacking cough interspersed within her speech.

'Sure, Granny May, I'll give you a lift back to your place, no problem.' She felt pity for her.

The old woman climbed on to the coach with some difficulty and tried to make herself feel comfortable, sitting next to Anna. With a full bag laden with fruit, the elderly woman continued to complain as they drove off in the direction of Granny's home.

'Oh, dear me, it's a hard life, Mrs Henderson,' she groaned, still coughing away. 'When old age begins to take hold, and jumps on your humpy back, this is when you become a good for nothing, ugly, worthless piece of junk. Are you listening to what I'm telling you?'

Anna nodded in agreement to Granny's negative tirade about herself, but in reality, her mind was still transfixed upon her brief affair with Sam. Who was now talking with Elena at her place of business.

'There is a saying which circulates around the elderly community, which is that it's best to hit yourself on the head with a mallet and send yourself packing into the ground, where everyone will eventually end up one day. And I agree, they are absolutely right. For those who have committed numerous sins, they are sent to the King of Hell, to meet with the most honourable Lucifer. And those without sin, go on a different route to Heaven and return to the glory of his Holiness St Peter,' she continued.

'Oh Granny, please don't say things like that. You're still very much alive and kicking.' Anna emphasised and tried to cheer her up.

'Yes dear, at your age I also said the same thing, but unfortunately, we all will come to this stage in life,' Granny sadly pointed out. 'Ah, my child, you see, it feels as though I've been travelling around the world, but it seems my life story had ended before it has begun.'

¶

Gradually, Anna developed an interest in what the old lady was talking about.

'In fact, my life story could be compared to the famous tale about two women who had been locked up in jail for twenty years. The story goes that the women talked day and night about their promiscuous relationships. When their terms of conviction had expired, they started complaining to the prison authorities by means of excessive profanity and disgusting behaviour. One of the women prisoners even began to mock the guards. 'What, already, hah, you are idiots. Can't you see we are still talking and all you can do is kick us out, with nowhere to go.' The guards yelled for them to get out of here, 'your time's up, what's wrong with you?''

Anna laughed but said nothing.

'My dear, I've got something for you,' Granny May said and took out an apple from her heavy bag. Without a moment's thought, she rubbed it on her dirty shirt and gave it to Anna.

'Take it, have a bite, it will do wonders for your tastebuds.'

Anna looked and reluctantly took the apple, sized it up, and took a big bite.

'You see my dear; it's tasty, isn't it?' the old lady asked, a sense of tension hanging in the air.

'Yes, it is, thank you,' Anna replied.

'Well, the fruit growers really try hard to make the apples they create, tasty for their community in which they live. Do you know what they did? They used all sorts of manures from horse, cow, sheep, pigs, chicken, bird and even human too. They then added some mouldy kitchen waste and veggie scraps into this mix. We feed these plants with every foul thing we can throw at them and as a result, Mother Nature gives us a fragrant sweet apple, but with us humans, it's the opposite! The more you feed us with wealth and luxury, the more rotten and loathsome we become, and this is a God-given, harsh fact of life.'

Anna suddenly felt nauseous after listening to this latest tale and quickly stopped eating the apple. Like the old witch in the Snow White fairy tale, Granny offered Anna another, but this time. she politely refused. Her passenger kept babbling on about nothing.

'You see, dear child, the whole world is rotten like manure. Look around and you'll notice all of what I've spoken about so far. For example, a handsome young man was following behind an old woman, if you could call her that. She was more like a skeleton really, with short skinny legs and needed to support herself by using a walking frame. Oftentimes, she could be found coughing and was often breathless as a result. Sensing she was being followed and before she walked through her front door, she turned and stared at the man and fearfully- asked who he was. He requested if he could go in and drink some water, as he was thirsty. And once inside, then demanded she lift her skirt and pull down her pants, so he could take a real close look at what she had between her legs. She could do nothing except to comply with his demand, as she was fearful for her life if she did not. And that is the kind of world we live in today, and it's getting worse, whether you want to acknowledge it or not. It is indeed a nasty place,' Granny May said happily, and took another chomp of the apple, which she chewed for some long length of time.

'Oh Granny, do you have any idea what happened after and who he was?' Anna asked impatiently. As for the poor unfortunate skeleton, Anna really didn't give a damn about her.

'Oh, Mrs Henderson, he was young, stupid, full of life, and who suffered from a long history of blackouts, I think? He grabbed whatever he could, when he could… In the name of the Holy Father, the Son and …' she crossed herself as she was relaying this pathetic story.

Even more curious now, Anna interrupted to ask Granny for a specific name.

'I have no idea, dear? If I had been the old woman, I surely would have known. For my age, my day is about to be written off and I'm thinking about another type of world that lies just beneath my feet.' Granny May replied and offered Anna another apple.

'Leave your apple for your family, Granny, and tell me more about the young man. What did he look like?' If nothing else, Anna was persistent.

'As far as physical appearance goes, he looked like any other normal average type of man. I see you're still young and interested. My dear, I know you and your family. You have a wonderful husband and beautiful son. Please keep your family together, for as long as you can,' Granny begged. Anna's mind was getting more and more restless with Granny's talk.

For a third time, Anna repeated the same question, in the hope of understanding better.

'I do remember he was tall, athletic build, handsome with a moustache. He always had a proper haircut, sweet talking and well-educated. His profession had something to do with the land. I think he lived somewhere in the city and was studying…'

'I don't believe it. It probably was him,' Anna said out loud without even noticing she had said it, as her tortured mind turned towards the direction of Sam.

'Yes, my dear, it was him,' Granny said, not fully understanding what she was really confirming.

A black curtain of despair lay in front of Anna's eyes. She clenched her jaw and tried to hide her face, which went a paler shade of white with fear. 'Yes, I knew it. He is a liar,' she spat out with anger, and quickly stopped the coach.

Granny looked at her. 'My dear, are you not feeling well?' she asked with compassion. 'You'll be okay,' and again offered Anna another apple. 'Please take it. It won't kill you!'

At this point, Anna burst into anger. 'Granny, for God's sake, I am fed up with everything, including your putrid apples!' She then hatefully stared at the old lady. 'If he was here right now, I'd run him over with the coach and happily watch him die as my horses trampled over him. Damn him to Hell.'

'Oh, my goodness, judging by your words and behaviour, you are absolutely right, as you stand faithful. I see you're most definitely the Lord's child and he will bless you! Dear Anna, your name will never be spoiled and scandalised ever. I wish everyone in this world was more like you, where all can once again blossom with luck, prosperity, happiness, and love. Our Lord in Heaven would cry great tears of joy and happiness to see this happen,' Granny May praised Anna dearly.

No longer of sound mind, Anna didn't even hear Granny's words of support. After a while though, she got over the initial bout of anger. 'Granny, tell me one last thing. When did all this happen with that man and the skeleton of an old woman?' she asked, with nervous trepidation, near ready to explode.

'Oh, dear child, it took place when I was a little girl and you would not even have been born then,' she informed.

Anna stared in shock at Granny, coupled with a huge question mark on her face. 'You're talking about something which happened a long time ago and you're not talking about today?' she asked incredulously.

'Yes dear, I'm talking about then, which for me feels like yesterday. Life moves on too fast, as does the blinking of an eye,' Granny May confirmed.

'Oh no,' Anna groaned and slammed her forehead with an open palm. She then bent her head forward and started to cry silently, her hat falling on to the seat between them.

'Oh Lord, what a beautiful hat, dropped from Heaven. You are one lucky woman, it suits you very much,' she exclaimed.

Shocked and bitterly disappointed to discover Sam was innocent of the atrocities Granny May had just been talking about, Anna was pushed further towards the edge of insanity, where her mind and soul were left floundering in eternity.

Granny took advantage of the situation and promptly swooped on Anna's hat and put it on her own head, thinking it may suit her better and make her look young again. 'My husband never liked me wearing different hats. While drunk, he used to hit me with his fist on top of my head and always forced me to wear the same one of his choice. For years, I did what I was told. As for him hitting me, I grew numb to his blows, but am still alive to tell the tale.'

Anna could no longer bear listening to Granny's senseless chatter.

'Enough, I've heard enough!' she mindlessly yelled at her. 'I don't want to hear your pointless stories anymore.' Anna swung the whip high in the air in order to get the horses moving again. For a few seconds, the animals reared up on their hind legs, before crashing back down again to run free and fast like the wind.

This caused Granny to further lose her balance, so tipped backwards and fell hard on top of the bag filled with apples. The bag burst open and the fruit went flying in all directions within the coach.

'Dear Lord, what are you doing, have you gone completely mental?' Granny cried but Anna ignored the stupid old biddy.

She kept travelling with her coach at the speed of light. People in town were stunned to see them and tried to figure out what was going on. Anna continued to torture her horses and hissed like a snake. 'I feel so cheated. I feel so useless. Oh, what a cruel world this is,' she muttered while the coach was going up and down over large rocks in the road and swinging dramatically from side to side.

Granny, having still lost her seat, could be seen at the back, jumping around like a rubber ball, turning and rolling with the apples.

'Good Lord my child, stop this instant. I want to get off!

What evil has been born within you, please stop!' Granny May kept screaming, coughing, sneezing, and gasping for breath.

After a while of this crazy journey into Hell, Anna eventually slowed as she approached Granny's house and finally did as Granny requested.

'Thank God, I've arrived home safely,' Granny May slurred her words, while crossing herself, ever so grateful her heart was still pumping. 'Oh dear, just look at my apples,' she cried to see such devastation.

'Granny, shut your mouth up at once about your damn apples, your home, your stories, and your freedom. Just get out of my coach and leave me alone.'

Granny collected what apples she could with shaking hands and climbed off the carriage, trying to ignore Anna's hurtful parting words. 'My good child, would you like one of the better ones before I go?' she asked, as Granny could see Anna was still in a great deal of anguish and pain.

'I said, shut up will you. Leave me alone,' Anna yelled, whipped the horses again to the inch of their life, and left in a flurry of dust.

Granny, with Anna's red hat still on her head, stood in front of her own house in complete disbelief. She didn't even notice the two women standing behind her.

'Oh, is that you, Mrs May? We didn't recognise you,' one of the women called out.

Granny turned around. 'Oh Lord, you scared me. I'm just May, not Mrs May,' Granny explained, trying to deny the fact that she was still married as the two women started laughing at her.

'Oh yes, we now see your life long wish has now come true. You finally bought yourself a new hat,' they mentioned, ignoring the business about Granny's title.

'A hat, what hat? You mean this? Oh, dear me, what have I done?' she asked, confused and then remembered. She then quickly took it off her head, fully realising it did not belong to her, but later changed her mind and quickly stuffed it into her bag. Upon entry, she made sure to hide it swiftly from her drunkard husband. *He must never ever see this beautiful hat! I must not ever wear it in front of him, except when he's not here or late at night when it's dark and he is asleep,* Granny thought and smiled. It would be her little secret.

¶

Soon after, a devastated Anna arrived at her own place, only to find Adrian was already there.

'Oh Adrian, how come you're already home?' she asked, with surprise.

'I had been patiently waiting, but when you didn't show up, I decided to walk. It was easy- but tell me, what happened? Why didn't you come and get me?' he asked with all innocence.

'I'm so sorry. I experienced a little mishap on the road, but don't worry, it won't ever happen again,' she mentioned and proceeded to remove the brand-new hat.

'Oh no, where is it?' she screeched in horror and then remembered Granny. *Oh no, not her! The smart old witch. On purpose, she kept talking continuously to distract me and then stole my beautiful red hat at my lowest moment. She's not as dumb as she looked. Oh well, I've still got my old hat and that's some-thing,* Anna lamented.

Chapter 11

'It's such a pity that in two more weeks, Sam's going back to university and there's no indication he will return. I thought we'd have plenty of time to speak to each other about agronomy and other agricultural stuff but unfortunately, that is not to be the case,' Peter quietly mentioned to his wife.

Anna cautiously listened to him whilst standing near the hallway mirror, planning her next move. She put on her old hat and addressed Peter. 'Yes, Elena told me Sam would be leaving soon to return to his studies.'

Peter became concerned, biting his lip and shaking his head. She was observing him in the mirror and hoped that Peter wanted to forgive. *Or maybe it's some kind of a trick? Does he really know everything about Sam and me? Peter is such a weak excuse of a human being, where Sam is a real man. You can never be like him, Peter. Never in a million years. Sam talks to win hearts, where each word is filled with a strong sense of love, hope, and pleasure. Peter, you don't understand me, my needs, my desire to be loved, hugged, touched, kissed and much more. You, Peter, know only one kind of language – 'I'm tired, it's late, next time and soon.'*

'Anna, you just mentioned that Elena said that Sam was leaving soon? Did you go and see her at the shop?' he asked, but she was too preoccupied with her own negative thoughts about her husband that she didn't hear a word he uttered.

She briefly came out of her own world of make-believe, only when he repeated the question. 'Oh yes, I was there just the other day and he had already visited to let her know of this fact.'

Peter had known Sam was going to see Elena in the shop, and was happy to know he did that. Maybe he could still become my brother-in-law one day, which would be quite incredible. In the meantime, Peter hoped his wife would not poke her nose in where it was not wanted and try to break them apart. This possibility really worried him. Sam however was smart and knows what was happening around him, and still managed to keep his cool. So, Peter decided to follow suit. His behaviour towards his wife remained cautious though. He began talking about the lovely clothes she was wearing, to make her happy, in order to divert her attention towards him, rather than interfering with the love life between Sam and Elena.

❡

After a couple of wild and woolly days on the river, Peter returned home from work, completely exhausted and drained. He washed his hands and joined his family for dinner.

'Ah, I probably had the worst twenty-four hours on the job so far. What a God-awful day it's been. The wind was brutally strong.

I thought my ferry would break off from the steel cable- and with myself onboard, it would sink into the raging waters. I stayed battling with the swirling currents and luckily, the ferry was saved from destruction thanks to the Lord,' he exclaimed with relief.

Adrian listened with interest and began wondering. 'Dad, please tell me- what would have happened if your ferry had broken away from the cables? Would you have jumped into the water and swum for dear life, or would you have stayed on the ferry and yelled for help?'

Peter shook his head. 'Well son, in such a dangerous set of circumstances, nobody can ever truly know what's going to happen ahead of time and how they would react. And it's in those few split seconds after the event, when your intuition kicks in and makes the decision for you.'

'Oh Dad, that is fast. Not even a second, wow! But what happens after that split second?' Adrian continued.

'You choose between life and death, depending on the decision your brain makes at the time. But to say this, is not entirely correct either. It is actually our Lord and master, who makes that final decision for us,' Peter tried to explain and firmly hugged Adrian.

'Dad, when I become a big king, I will look after you from my rock on top of the waterfall. I won't let you get into any trouble. I will save you.'

This is when Anna entered the conversation, asking about the rock.

'It is the biggest rock that you can see at the top of the world,' Adrian answered.

'Ah, I give up,' she said, throwing her hands in the air with exasperation. 'It's nothing but a kid's stupid fantasy.' And left them to their little game to get some food from the kitchen. Of course, Anna conveniently chose to forget that Adrian was still just a child.

¶

A week later, just before bedtime, Peter told Anna the news that he was going to be busy moving his mother, Regina, from her old place to a new one.

'I've already notified my customers that the ferry will not be running on those two days of the transfer. In fact, my mother is going to move not far from the place where I now work.'

Anna was surprised to hear this, as she had been given no prior knowledge that this was to happen.

'I'll go and give her a hand to get things ready initially, and then put all her stuff on the ferry, to take it across to her new home the following day,' he informed Anna of his plan. As far as he was concerned, this signalled the finish of their conversation and so left the room to ready himself for bed.

He popped his head to look in on Adrian first though. 'My son, remember your father before going to sleep tonight,' he said, as part of their nightly ritual.

'Don't worry, Dad, I'll be thinking of you,' he said and promptly crawled into bed.

While lying down, Adrian began to think again about the coolest rock on Earth. In his fantasy, he was standing in his mysterious, invisible house made of glass. Soon, he entered the dream space and began talking in his sleep. 'I am the almighty king. My invisible palace is where I rule the whole world. Please listen, dear subjects, for your powerful king who speaks these words to you.'

¶

While Adrian was having this lovely dream, his mum's mind was filled with harrowing thoughts that kept her wide awake. As a result, she quietly came out of the bedroom, scheming and plotting her next move, which needs to be taken soon. In her possessed state of mind, she began to imagine how she would take revenge upon Sam. She always believed that he had to be hers only, and no one else could have him- *but as he's now seeing Elena as well! He needs to be punished for his sin of being unfaithful to me.* She would meet with him for one final time, and do something he would never forget.

With that sorted, Anna continued to wander through the house, looking like a lost ghost. She looked awfully untidy, and wore a sad face. Hair in wild disarray like an untamed lioness, eyes red and full of tears, while saliva dripped from her mouth. Her entire body was shaking, and she could hardly stand up straight. She stared at her reflection for a while, and suddenly grabbed her head and screamed. Thankfully for her, was not loud enough to wake the household. She then asked the mirror, 'who is that old bag standing before me? Oh no, surely it can't be me, can it?'

In horrified shock, she ran towards another room which had no mirror, dropped to her knees and wondered what compelled her to do and think such evil thoughts.

¶

Next morning, Peter woke up all cheerful like, ate a hearty breakfast, and readied to begin this new day of helping his mother.

'Well, my dear family, it's time for me to go and do my good deed for the next couple of days.' He bent low to kiss Anna, but she did not respond to his gesture in any way. 'And you, my son, be sure to be on your best behaviour for your mother and remember what your dad has also taught you to do,' Peter reminded him.

'Yes, Dad. And I'll be sure to think of you while you are away,' he said, happily giving his dad a hug. Peter said his final goodbyes and departed in a hurry.

On the way to Regina's place, he pondered about how to utilise this day in the best way possible. His mother was happy to see him finally arrive.

'It's so wonderful to see you son,' she said, while welcoming him home.

'My dear mother, I'm always happy to see you and assist in any way I can, you know that,' he replied. 'So, where and when do we begin?'

¶

Today was definitely not Anna's day and felt glad when her husband left to help his mother. She felt strange and unhappy, her face pale due to lack of sleep. Even Adrian got scared when he saw her that morning.

Oh no, what's happened to my mum? She looks quite different today, why is she acting like that? 'Mum, you look quite frazzled. I think you need a rest. Please go back to bed and have a proper sleep. I'll go to school by myself.'

'Oh, no can do. I will drop you off at the halfway mark. Then you go the rest of the way to school while I come back home to get some much-needed rest, as you have suggested,' she explained with half a lie, continuing to get ready.

'Mum, are you sure?' Adrian asked anxiously, and she stressed there was no problem in doing so. Even though he remained uncertain, he continued getting ready for school.

Anna wore the same dress she'd had on the day she and Sam met for the first time. She decided to dress down and took on a more peasant look. On her uncombed and unwashed hair, she wore her old hat, but this time, did not wear makeup, brooch, lipstick, perfume, gloves, or jewellery. She looked completely different- near dowdy in fact, and took her black handbag with her for the first time.

Anna and her son sat on the coach. Adrian mischievously looked back at their home and said, 'goodbye, House! I'll be back real soon,' and waved.

'Yes, bye bye, House,' Anna sadly whispered and away they went, mother and son, on their own separate missions.

During the trip, Adrian kept glancing at his unusually quiet mother from time to time and kept wondering, *why is she so different today? What's wrong with her? What's happening?* All these thoughts made him cuddle up closer to her. This is when he moved Anna's handbag.

She glanced briefly at Adrian and her handbag, but said nothing.

¶

This time, Anna was completely absent from reality and acted strangely cool, with no smile, no words, and no questions for her son. Adrian was near her, but she was psychologically far apart from him and he could sense this. Because his mother would not communicate with him, Adrian was forced to use his own imagination to fill in the gaps as to the reason why his mother was acting so weird on this particular day. *Perhaps she does not love me anymore, or maybe I'm ugly and too childish for her to deal with. But she is still my mother and I love her dearly, whatever dark mood she was in.*

Anna stopped at a cross road. She closed her eyes momentarily and took an intake of breath. 'Well Adrian, we're finally here and it is time for us to separate. You are going to school, while I must fulfil an important job before I can go home and rest,' she mentioned with an insensitive voice.

Adrian sat on the coach for an unusually long time. He did not want to leave her. He looked longingly at his mother, tears trickling down his cheeks from his beautiful chocolate brown eyes. 'Please, Mum, I know there's something wrong. Can you tell me what it is?' he asked.

Anna remained silent, feeling quite unperturbed and untouched by his tears.

'Mum, please! Talk to me,' he said sweetly, hoping to also receive a kiss before parting, but she just looked at him without reacting.

Failing to hold her composure any longer, she finally hugged and kissed Adrian lightly on the cheeks.

He immediately responded by giving her a big hug and kiss as well. 'I love you, Mum,' he whispered to her. 'Do you love me?'

She looked at him with watery eyes. All she could do was nod and hoped it would be enough for her son to accept.

'Mum, I have to go now,' he said and came down off the coach. Whilst dismounting, he accidentally knocked over Anna's handbag, which fell to the ground, unopened.

'Adrian, watch out! Can you be more careful? See what you've done? That's my handbag, and there are lots of important things in there which little children should not see. Do you understand?' she yelled at him unnecessarily.

In shock and fear, he retrieved the bag and promptly returned it to her. 'I'm sorry, Mum. It won't happen again,' he apologised sincerely. 'When I become a big King, I will be sure to look after you and dad. For today, a new King shall be born into this world,' he assured her with his child-like mind.

She comprehended nothing of what her son was saying, and because she was still so absentminded, Anna did not bother to comment.

'Mum, when will I see you again?' he asked. After waiting a bit and receiving no response and because it was getting late, he simply waved and left.

Anna inhaled a deep sigh of relief and madly yelled at the horses, 'take me away!'

And once again, gave them instruction to run towards their rental property. Full of anger, shame, and revenge, she intended to give Sam her final word. She arrived looking quite dishevelled and breathless.

Vivien was the only one at the house, while Martin was in the field, doing whatever he does best, and Sam was once again in town.

As Vivien peered through the window, she saw someone quickly running towards the house. At first, she did not recognise the dirty individual, but realised it was Anna.

'Is that Anna Henderson? Surely it can't be,' she said out loud. 'Oh, my Lord, it is her. Something awful must have happened,' she exclaimed as Anna quickly approached the entrance.

'Hello, Lady Henderson,' Vivien greeted her guest.

Anna stood in the open doorway, quite hypnotised and confused as she busily kept looking around. It seemed to Vivien she was afraid of something, noticing the black handbag and whip she carried. They shook violently in Anna's trembling hands.

Her outward appearance also stunned Vivien to the core. Without wanting to sound judgmental, she could not believe how Anna looked so appalling. Her hat hung madly on the side of her head, her dress was all crinkled, dust layered her face, and her eyes were fiercely bloodshot. As well as this, Anna looked agitated, nervous, and was behaving very strangely.

'Please come in, Lady Henderson,' Vivien invited, but Anna did not budge an inch.

'Is … is he at home?' Anna struggled to express her words, still looking around.

'Who are you talking about, dear?' Vivien asked, unsure of who she was referring to.

'Him! Your son, Sam!' Anna said more clearly.

'Oh, I see,' Vivien said, with puzzlement that pertained to Anna's real intent for asking the question. 'Lady Henderson, he is not here. What's happened? Can you tell me about it?' Vivien asked with anxious concern.

'Mrs Vivien, do you know when he will return?' Anna asked and squeezed her handbag even tighter.

'My dear lady, I don't know when he'll be back. Why do you ask?' she enquired.

'I just want to know when,' Anna replied, tapping the whip nervously on her handbag. Her rate of breathing quickened and was now most audible.

Vivien looked at Anna's handbag with a bewitched expression on her face and asked, 'oh, dear lady, I see you've got an exceptionally nice bag with you this time. It's so lovely. It must be brand new, as I have not noticed it before.'

Anna was not interested in her worthless words. 'Do you know where I can find him?' Anna demanded.

'Lady Henderson, please understand when I say that this is a difficult question for a mother to answer.' Vivien was unsure as to how she should respond to her unwelcome question about Sam, and started wondering why she was so interested about him, and behaving in an unusual manner. 'My lady, Sam's vacation is coming to an end very soon and after tomorrow, he will be returning to university to continue his study,' Vivien informed her. 'All he told me this morning was that he intended to visit the ferry, so he could bid your husband farewell. In fact, there is a real possibility he might be there right now.'

Vivien was keen to uncover the reason as to why she was so determined to see Sam? 'Please, come inside. We can then converse more freely with each other,' she said, in an attempt to find out the real motive behind Anna's persistence, in wanting to know of Sam's whereabouts.

'Here or inside, it makes no difference to me,' Anna said haughtily, but soon changed her mind and went inside. 'Mrs Vivien, the reason for my visit today is because I wanted to ask Sam or your husband, whether they have found my original lost brooch yet,' she said, blatantly lying through her teeth.

'Oh dear, I remember you said you had one- I mean, *lost* one,' Vivien stuttered.

'Original always means original,' Anna mentioned.

'Of course, my dear, I'm totally at a loss as to what could have happened to your valuable piece of jewellery. Surely, it must be of great sentimental value to you,' she sadly replied. 'My lady, I promise that I will keep searching for your lost brooch until I find it,' Vivien pronounced.

'Hmm, yes, yes… that's fine,' Anna grumbled and went to fix her hat.

Vivien offered her a seat, but she refused. What an interesting but weird woman. *Why is she acting so different today? Is the brooch the reason why she's here or has she really come to see my son, Sam?* With this new and unexpected insight, Vivien began to mentally replay all of Anna's visits to date. She started seeing observable patterns, such as that every visit after the first, Peter did not accompany Anna. Secondly, she noted Anna had spent time with Sam alone when both she and her husband were not at home. As well as the fact that with all her visits, Anna kept eluding to Sam in one way or another, and especially the fact that at each occurrence, she appeared aesthetically more pleasing to the eye- except of course, for today. As Vivien compiled this information together in her head into a cohesive and chronological sequence, what she had previously thought to be separate, unrelated events were indeed not. And at last, she was able to piece the picture of Anna together. Surely, her son was not so reckless to want her in his company in a physical sense, especially since she is a married woman with a husband and young son.

'Well, I have to go now. You have told me what I needed to know,' she said whilst trying to muster up the strength to put a smile on her face, no matter how disdainful it was for her to do so.

All of a sudden, an unexpectedly loud bang and hissing sound could be heard, which frightened both women. Vivien immediately realised the origin of the noise and rushed quickly to the kitchen.

A hot pot of soup, which had been boiling boisterously, lost its lid due to a build-up of overwhelming pressure. The contents of which, like an active volcano, gushed over the edge and onto the flaming stove.

'Oh no, my soup has boiled over,' Vivien exclaimed in a mad panic and ran as fast as she could to the kitchen. 'Oh, what a mess. I'll need to clean it up immediately.'

While Vivien was dealing with the latest household calamity, and with her guest showing a total lack of compassion and concern for her host's crisis, Anna thought, *what a dumb peasant woman she is. She can keep her lousy soup. All I want is Sam.* And promptly left the property.

The next time Vivien turned around, she realised Anna had already left the building. *Oh, dear me, I wanted to offer her some snacks to eat on the way home, but it's too late, she's gone.* Vivien was worried about her despite the present dilemma she was in, and shook her head in dismay.

¶

Further along the road, an alienated Anna travelled with a sense of urgency, as if she was an escaped convict pursuing a helpless victim, only murder on her mind. In this case, the intended target was Sam. She felt like a bald eagle, determined to tear defenseless Sam from limb to limb with its devastating claws. Whilst travelling, enraged yet decisive, words came to her foggy mind. *This time, he will be forever mine. He will be there, because I know Peter is at his mother's place. So naturally,*

Sam will be awaiting Peter at the ferry. This is the opportunity to settle the score between him and me once and for all. Sam, I'm coming for you… And like an expert sharp shooter, she calculated the exact punishment he deserved.

Chapter 12

Earlier in the morning, when Anna had taken her son halfway to school, Adrian used his mother's carelessness to his advantage. Anna, oblivious to the world around her, didn't think that Adrian would ever avoid going to school. Her beloved son had other plans and took the opportunity to visit Steve, who lived nearby.

Upon arriving at his fellow classmate's home, and because Adrian was badly puffing and panting, he blurted out, 'hey Steve, do you know what?'

'Tell me! What?' his friend hurriedly asked.

'Today's an excellent day and we should go somewhere different and exciting,' Adrian insisted.

'Oh yes, but what about school?' Steve asked in a more serious tone.

'School, what's that?' Adrian laughingly replied. 'Listen, I've never been absent before, so my teacher will forgive me for not being there just this once. When he questions me tomorrow, I'll simply give an excuse such as I was sick. My leg was sore or something similar. He'll believe me. No problems.'

'Oh, Adrian, that sounds like a plausible excuse. Even I

would believe it,' Steve responded, in joint cahoots with his buddy. 'So, tell me, what's your plan for the day? Where exactly are we going?'

'We are going to the most amazing waterfall with a rock on top,' he replied with growing excitement. 'And on top of that huge rock, is an invisible glass house,' he whispered.

Steve wondered and commented, 'it must be nice to live in a glass house. Oh goody. Hey Adrian, I like your plan, so let's not waste any more time and get there real fast. In fact, you know what, we will be back before school finishes and our parents won't even know where we've been. Oh yes, this is such a great idea of yours.'

'I promised my dad I will be a big king, and if I yelled loudly from inside the transparent glass house, he'll hear me from the ferry. Isn't that something else?' Adrian declared.

'Wow, you'll be the king. Will I be able to hear you as well?' Steve asked.

'Yes, and you can be the king's assistant if you want,' Adrian happily proposed.

'Wow, gee! I can be your assistant. I can't believe it. Let's go,' Steve responded to Adrian's plan.

'I know the exact location, as I've been there before with my parents. I tell you, it's such a wonderful place, right on top of the world,' Adrian clarified.

'Oh wow, that sounds simply wonderful. I've never been there myself, but I would love to go,' Steve confirmed positively to his friend's optimistic description.

'But you have to remember one important thing though.

There can only ever be one king to rule the world, and that will be me,' Adrian accentuated this particular command.

'Okay, I don't have a problem with that. I understand,' Steve replied. 'Now please tell me, my king, how far away is this magical place?'

'If we were to run now, we would reach there soon. However, if we rode our push bikes, we would have reached there by now,' Adrian pointed out.

'Hmm, then what do we have to do?' Steve worriedly asked. 'Oh yes, I know.' He suddenly remembered and said, 'I've got two small bikes out the back, which we can use to get there really quick!'

With this suggestion, they wasted no time in finding the bikes, rode to their agreed destination, and arrived shortly thereafter.

'Oh gee, wow!' Steve exclaimed, as he couldn't believe the beauty of what he was seeing. 'Oh Adrian, this is amazing. You are an absolute genius to have discovered it. Oh, look at that, there is so much water. Tell me though, where is the glass house?' Steve anxiously asked.

'You see that impressive looking rock on top of the water-fall?' Adrian said as he pointed towards the general direction. 'That's where it is.'

'But ... but I can't see it,' Steve asked, perplexed and curious.

'You can't see it because it's made out of glass, silly,' Adrian answered with confidence.

'Oh, I thought it might still be visible to the eye,' Steve replied.

'Even when you arrive right on top of it, you still can't see it and only I can touch it,' Adrian continued. 'It is there, in that invisible magical house, I will become the king. The grand master of the world, land, sea, forest and people- including you,' Adrian emphasised.

'Oh, thank you, my big king.' Steve was ecstatic as his friend included him in his grand plan.

'I'm His Majesty, the king, and everyone will bow down and listen to me,' Adrian warned him.

'Well, Your Majesty, tell me: will our teacher listen?' Steve asked with intelligence.

'Of course he will! Everybody will,' Adrian repeated.

'That's good to know, Your Majesty. For once, our teacher will listen to us instead of us listening to him,' Steve laughingly replied.

¶

Massive amounts of flowing water separated at the rock's edge and circulated through its circumference to create an enormous waterfall. The thundering of water on water was a glowing testament to the magnificence of this natural phenomenon.

Adrian and Steve now approached the spot, and had difficulty communicating. It was so loud, they had to shout to hear each other.

In order to stand on the rock, Adrian and Steve were required to travel across a thick log. It had fallen and remained positioned, perpendicular to the river's edge despite the force of water which were being exerted upon it. A healthy tree at one stage, it now served as a bridge for the boys, connecting the river's edge to the rock. Being half-submerged under water for such a long period of time, the wood was now covered in layers of moss, which made it dangerously slippery. This meant they had to be very careful where they put their feet.

Brimming with excitement, Adrian was determined to fulfill his childhood fantasy of becoming the most powerful person in the world, the almighty Majesty, the king.

Adrian screamed over the thunderous rapids, 'Steve, I'm going across the river. Doing so will enable me to touch the invisible glass house and in turn, allow me to be king, but you can't come any further. Do you hear me?'

'Yes, yes, I hear you, I'll return to the bank of the river and wait for you there,' Steve replied.

'I'll be back a little later,' Adrian yelled.

'Yes, Your Majesty. I shall see you upon your return,' Steve called out.

Adrian continued to climb the dead tree. Somewhat cautiously, Adrian went to balance himself, by holding on to the branches. Water rose and fell and banged itself on the sides, splashing all over him. It became more treacherous to get across to the flat rock, as massive swirls of water rushed over with a huge thundering noise. Adrian lost his grip and fell into a pool of water that lay close below, which led into faster water that continued the journey. After a lot of struggle, he finally managed to swim opposite to the flow and reached the mystery rock from a slightly different direction. He stood there in that mesmerised state, thinking it must be all a mirage. He wondered and looked around before realising he was really standing on the rock he intended to do for so long now, since he first saw this place.

Wow… oh my Lord, is this the invisible glass house my dad told me about? Oh, what a beauty. No roof, no walls, no floor, no windows, no door, no nothing. Just pure emptiness in nothing! It's a house without a house. Oh wow, I'm at the top of the world. Adrian stood still for a respectful minute and suddenly, he screamed a single key word at the top of his lungs.

This was immediately followed by a pin drop of silence, when the word 'Me!' began to echo and reverberate in all directions, multiplying its own sound, before eventually fading away. Oh, what an amazing experience this is. Adrian kept yelling, 'behold the big king. I am the Almighty King!' Echoes kept bouncing backward and forwards. The drizzling noise of water added its own special music to his voice, and he continued to shout, 'I am the grand master of the entire world!'

Standing in his invisible home, Adrian felt as if he were living his dream as this physical reality quickly slipped from his mind. 'Oh, how beautiful it is to be here!' he exclaimed.

'Adrian, where are you?' Steve bellowed, confused as to where his friend's voice was precisely coming from before it reached his ears.

Paying little attention to Steve's urgent calls, Adrian continued to speak out loudly. 'Dad, Dad! Come to me, Dad! Listen to your son. I am now king of the whole world, which I've always wished to be. Are you happy for me? Do you hear my voice? I love you, Dad, I love you, Mum.'

Those distinct words echoed through the nearby valley, forests and river that surrounded the small town of Plymouth.

¶

After what seemed like an extended period of time, an exhausted Adrian started returning to the present and began to depart the sanctuary of the rock, towards Steve who had been patiently waiting.

Despite the immediate danger of slipping on the log before plummeting to his death, Adrian was able to navigate his way back to safety, where his friend was standing.

'Oh Adrian, quickly tell me about your experience. What was it like inside the glass house?' Steve demanded impatiently. 'Oh Adrian, I would love to touch the glass house myself. Can I?'

'No, you can't go,' Adrian adamantly refused. 'Remember, I am the one and only king, and only I can stand within its invisible walls,' Adrian replied, exaggerating every syllable as he pointed to himself in order to clearly convey his superiority.

'But, but ... I want to go where you have been,' Steve insisted.

'No, I warned you at the very beginning. Don't you remember? If you go without my permission, you will never come back alive. You could drown and disappear without anyone ever knowing. Do you understand me?' And repeated his warning with a stern voice.

'Oh well, I won't go then. As you are the almighty king and as I am your obedient servant, I will obey your orders,' Steve replied obediently, feeling somewhat rejected.

g

The two young boys spent the rest of the afternoon playing games, still totally captivated and spellbound by this enchanting environment. While Adrian continued to feel an ethereal aura resonating from the invisible glass house, still majestically sitting within his sight.

CHAPTER 13

Meanwhile, Peter was still at his mother's place. By the afternoon, everything had been packed away. Taking a well-earned breather, Peter and his mother shared a pleasant lunch together.

In conversation, Regina touched on an emotional subject about her life. 'Peter, I have nothing against you and Elena. After all, a child is still a child and they are innocent bystanders who can sometimes witness the differences of ideals and opinions between both parents. Of course, it is not right to talk about your late father in any negative way but ...' Shortly after, his mother started weeping.

Peter tried his best to comfort her by giving her a warm hug. 'Oh. Mum, please don't cry. We must be happy and strong with our own love for each other,' he suggested.

'Oh yes, that's true, my son,' she proclaimed and gave a quaint smile.

Realising the time was fast slipping away from him, he said, 'I have to go back home now, but tomorrow, I'll return to transport you to your new abode.' Peter leaned across, kissed her, and left, feeling a great sense of achievement.

¶

Whilst on the road, he decided to alter his plans. He thought that going home would be a bit too far to travel when the ferry was so much closer. It made better sense to go direct to there instead and so decided that this is what he will do. Peter then remembered there was something else he had to do, before he could return to his second home away from home. He must buy a bouquet of special flowers, which would be a nice present for Sam and Elena. Oh yes, that would be a kind thing to do. Because she was the best sister ever and for Sam, it was to be a parting gesture, before he left for university. Secretly, he still hoped that one day, Sam would still become his brother-in-law.

After returning from the florist and arriving once again at the ferry, he decided to clean the entire place from top to bottom, so it could be clean and presentable when any visitors might come.

The whole day had been full of bright sunshine. Inside the cabin, he felt super calm, held prisoner in some heavenly paradise which only he could sense.

In spite of his recent heavy emotional suffering because of his wife's attraction to Sam, he was making every effort to forget about it all. In the hope that, when Sam returned to his studies, Anna would forget all about him and their marriage could continue moving forward, as if nothing ever happened.

Peter made himself some tea. Once completed, he went to sit in relaxation for a few treasured moments. His mind began to drift into a state of joy as he reflected upon his work as a ferry man. Whilst drinking slowly, he glanced towards the direction of the table and looked at the book sitting there.

Ah, yes, this is my father's book, called Job of Love. *I've always been curious to read it, but have never had a spare minute, until now.* And so, allowed himself to revisit a recent memory about his father and of his special request he made of his son, six months before he died.

'Dear son of mine, one day when you get the time, please read this special book. I know you'll love it.'

The book talked about the history of the previous owner of the ferry before it was transferred into the capable hands of the Henderson family.

After taking another sip of his now lukewarm tea, Peter began to read. But because of the balmy warm breeze blowing on his face, he began to be lulled into a heavy state of drowsiness. He fought to stay awake, but could not.

He was concerned that if he should fall asleep now, it being late afternoon. He valiantly tried to shift his focus towards the contents of the book. However, his body was failing him, as it became weaker and more languid, as his hand slowly flexed towards his knee. The book dropped to the ground at the exact same page he had just finished reading and Peter slipped into a very deeply satisfied slumber, with his back to the cabin door. The chapter title was called 'The Beginning of a New Drama'. The vase of flowers, which he had bought for his sister and Sam, was situated close by, on the table near to where he was sitting.

❡

Near the waterfall, Adrian once again climbed on top of the big flat rock, retrying his imagination. With a high-pitched voice, he called out, 'Dad, Dad, where are you? Wake up and come to me. I love you, Dad. I am now king, do you hear me?' The tones bounced off the walls of nature with a clear resonance, distributed evenly across a large distance.

However, Peter remained oblivious to Adrian's calls.

As for Anna, she heard her son's voice but was unable to register it, as her fuzzy mind clouded with a myriad of conflicting emotions. Anna's fury proved stronger than her love for Adrian, and as a consequence, remained fixed in her own picture. Breathless and ruined, she arrived at the ferry and stood on the pier, petrified. She knew what needed to be done. *It's now or never.* She clutched her handbag harder to her chest before approaching.

She noticed the ferry rocked from side to side against the uneven ripples of water. Inside, Peter was blissfully dreaming about his loving family.

In the distance, pleading voices could still be heard. 'Dad, Mum! Come to me please. I love you both. Come and see your king.' The sounds entered the hull of the boat and pulsated throughout.

Peter regarded the source as part of the dream he was having, and feeling so enamoured, he spoke. 'Yes, yes, I do hear you, son. You are now the big king. I'm so proud of you.' Peter then once again lapsed into sleep mode. In fact, he was near comatose with exhaustion.

Meanwhile, Anna boarded the ferry and cautiously begins

to approach the cabin. She stopped outside the door, her hand-bag still firmly held close to her body. With a few quick glances in all directions, she ensured that nobody was watching before she entered.

The door opened with a screech, which emanated from the rusty hinges. Anna carefully tried not to make any more noise than what she needed, and observed the half-reclining body sitting in the chair. Proceeding slowly with her analysis, she found a side table supporting a half-finished cup of something and a vase of beautiful flowers, and a book lying open on the ground, near his feet.

Anna's focus quickly returned to the floral display. *How dare he buy her flowers,* she thought in great disgust. Shrouded with insanity, she took a deep breath, her resolve for revenge intensifing. Spontaneously, the seemingly unrelated voice heard earlier rang through her suppressed consciousness. This made her feel disorientated, resulting in her falling to the ground and hitting her head with some force.

When she recovered, she found the human figure remained unmoved in his chair. She walked closer with the black hand-bag held in front of her, as though it was a source of protection.

'Sam,' she whispered softly. 'I found you. Yes, Peter is at his mother's place. I know you were waiting for him, but I'm here instead. Sam, I am yours and you are mine. You love me, and I love you. Do you remember the time when you promised I would be your wife? You are avoiding me because you lust after that evil bitch, Elena. Sam, do you know what you've done? You thoroughly destroyed me and now I'm nothing.

Because of you, my beloved Peter now looks at me with disgust, as if I am nothing but an overripe tomato that he can simply stamp out of existence. This makes you evil as well. You remain silent because you feel guilty and I can now easily overlook that, because I brought you a present, which you so thoroughly deserve.'

With the completion of her verbal dressing-down, she swiftly pulled out a small revolver from the bag, pointed it close to the back of his head and without any hesitation whatsoever, pulled the trigger.

The deafening sound of gunshot blasted through the room and quickly spread outwards, through the open doors and windows.

The sound of the gun happened in perfect synchronicity with Adrian's demand for his parents to join him. Anna knew the shot had been fatal, and the recipient of her unexpected parting gift was dead. She allowed herself a moment of joyful release, pleased with the outcome of the revenge she so successfully committed and gave a tiny smile of accomplishment.

Without looking back, she calmly walked outside and put her still smoking revolver into her handbag. She stood contemplating her recent actions, but even now her anger continued, and she held a conversation with the dead man she once loved.

'Sam, you're the worst liar in the world,' Anna uttered, as she tightly clenched her jaw. 'These are my final words. You welcomed me into your home and made love to me. A few days later, you promised to marry me, but you reneged and because of this elaborate lie you made up, I have decided this will be your final resting place,' she said mockingly, and laughed hysterically.

In order to hide the evidence, she carefully detached the docking cables, and soon after, strong currents pulled the ferry further into the river, heading straight for complete annihilation. No body, no case, no charge. As far as Anna was concerned, she had carried out the perfect crime of passion.

¶

Watching the tragedy further unfold, Anna's body quivered with delight at what she did. Her eyes were painted black and her disassociated mind caused her to experience an irreversible state of shock.

All Anna could do was stand there and wait for a sign. It seemed she'd lost the ability to think about anything anymore. In her shattered conscience, only hollow, horrible words materialised within her bedazzled brain. She knew with all her heart that Peter, her darling husband, would no longer love her any more. Not wanting to acknowledge this painful fact of life, she discontinued this particular awful thought.

¶

By chance, a man walking alongside the river canal saw the Henderson ferry detached from the dock, now freely floating down the river. The man became frantic and started to yell.

'Oh, dear Lord, the ferry's broken away from the dock. Please someone, anyone! Help me. The ferry has gone!'

At this instant, a second individual appeared. 'Hey man, why are you screaming? What's happened?'

'Look, the ferry has broken loose from its mooring,' the first man shouted in frustration, while pointing to the large structure swaying gently in the middle of the river.

'You mean that floating thing? Whose ferry does it belong to?' the second man asked in confusion.

'That is the Henderson's ferry over there,' the first man shouted in a great state of panic.

The two men shouted out loud in conjunction with each other. 'Help save the ferry! Quickly, help save the ferry!'

This triggered many people to come to their aid.

'What are you waiting for? Hurry up and do something. The ferry's getting swept down the river with every passing second,' the first man said, indicating its new location.

'Alright, I'll quickly get a boat,' another helpfully suggested.

Someone else also offered assistance as well. By now, many people were present at the scene, all trying in their own separate ways to save the only river transportation they had available.

'Oh, good Lord, that's impossible. The Henderson's ferry is gone,' could be heard many times, spoken amongst the crowd of shocked onlookers. Many congregated on the old dilapidated bridge- talking, yelling and pondering upon this devastating situation.

'Our ferry is gone, what will happen now?' the people asked, in dismay.

'Oh no, Henderson's ferry has sunk. What a complete catastrophe. Maybe the exterior frame was penetrated by something sharp,' someone loudly uttered in disbelief.

'But … but where is Peter? Does he know what's happening?' a caring person said, with concern. 'Quick, let's try and save him. He's surely trapped inside, screaming for help.'

'Yes, where is he? Did he manage to swim across to the other side or not?' another person enquired.

'Probably he was drunk as a skunk,' another yobbo maliciously commented.

But he was not the only one who stood around gossiping and speculating, and not being of any real use to anyone.

'The fire brigade and police are on their way. Did somebody call the doctor or Father Greene?' someone asked, trying to be more practical.

'Oh no, I can't believe it. Has our Peter gone down with the ferry?' somebody enquired.

'I heard a loud bang before. Maybe it was the sound of the cable breaking, or it could have even been a gunshot. Did anybody else hear that bang?'

'Oh hell, it's all a total mystery. How can such terrible things happen in our small community? Poor ferry man. It looks like he's gone to a watery grave. But what about his wife, Anna?' someone said, bringing up the possibility of the most delicate and sensitive issue of Peter's possible death.

'You mean the mystery rider in black boots?' a man queried.

Another third party answered, 'ah yes, you mean the witch? Well, it could be her.'

A huge commotion from the crowd erupted at this latest comment.

'I too am positive I heard a gunshot earlier,' a woman confirmed, sobbing her little heart out.

'You mean, it could have been murder? On that ferry in the middle of the river, which is swerving and swinging around like a drunk? But that's impossible! And even if it is, then the murderer must surely be dead too.' The conclusions kept on coming thick and fast, which made the matter even more critical.

Someone with a bit of common sense called out to those who had been speaking. 'And why don't you all mind your own business and shut up? Instead, you should be thinking about how we can save our ferry, rather than wasting time by throwing about wild stories and false accusations into thin air. You should be ashamed of yourselves. One small link of the chain could have snapped, and you automatically think revolver, canon, and bomb- or earthquake too. Just cool the theories for a bit. In fact, now that I think about it further, a nerve must have snapped in your brain, which is what you actually heard.'

'Hey, why don't you all stop yapping and run for proper assistance immediately,' another commanding voice boomed above the rest.

Many people continued going up and down the river bank in a blind panic, screaming helplessly. One of the people there urgently requested help again. 'Please, can anyone jump into the water to investigate the situation more closely? I can't go, I don't know how to swim.'

His words were ignored, as people started to home in and gossip about Roger, Peter's father, who had been their previous ferry man. 'Roger did not die. He faked his own death and left to become a priest in a nearby town and the person found on the ferry was either a cleaner or his assistant.'

'Please shut your mouth, you idiot. If you're not willing to present the facts as they really are, just go back to the tavern and keep yapping this nonsense to those other drunks like yourself.'

In the maddening throng, someone else started talking about Elena and of her budding romance with Sam. They suggested that perhaps Peter may not have liked Sam being the boyfriend of his sister and in defiance, Sam and Elena might have planned this present dilemma.

Another story soon broke out about how they recently saw Adrian at the waterfall, standing calmly on the rock, pleading for his father to come to him.

'How awful, if that's the truth. While Peter lies dying on the ferry, his son, from the top of the waterfall, is calling out to him.'

'It simply does not make any sense. Besides which, what does that all add up to?' one of the people from the crowd queried.

Near Elena's shop, one man ran in an unseeing stupor. 'Henderson's ferry is sinking, or it may have already gone under by now.'

Elena heard his crazy talk and without thinking, ran outside to question the man. 'What ferry? What do you mean?' Elena could not believe what she had just heard.

'Yes, yes, your brother's ferry,' the man uttered while making the sign of the cross.

Sam was in the shop with Elena at the time, and whispered to himself, 'oh Lord, what am I hearing? It can't possibly be.' In a flash, he quickly joined her on the street.

'Oh Sam, did you hear what that man just said?' Elena asked as she hugged him, needing comfort.

'Elena, we'll immediately go and see what's happened to Peter. Let's go.' Without delay, they both ran towards the river.

'Hey, what's happening? Why are you in such a hurry?' curious people questioned, while trying to stop them from leaving.

'We've been told the ferry's sinking! We're going there to see if we can save it.'

'Don't panic, girl. It's already been saved,' someone reported wrongly.

Ignoring this last comment, Elena and Sam wanted to see for themselves what the actual situation was but the ferry was not where it should have been. Further downstream, they could see it was busy swirling and twirling, getting hit from the debris which uncontrollably floated in its path.

Sam held Elena close, realising her fragile state of mind. 'Elena, think positive. Don't give up hope and don't think the worst. Everything will be alright. Trust me,' Sam said as he tried desperately to calm her anxious heart.

'Oh Sam, the ferry is gone,' she said, and collapsed into tears.

'Yes Elena, it is there, fighting with the waves. And we can do little to save it,' he said, feeling great sorrow while caressing and stroking her hair.

'Oh, my Lord no, we've lost our heritage. My brother will be devastated, and we need to make sure he hears about it- only from us.'

'Don't worry, Elena, we'll tell Peter together, later. Because I know he's presently safe at his mother's place, helping her to move,' Sam said, with some authority.

'Yes, I know we can't do much about the ferry and that human life is always more important.'

Somebody in the crowd then spoke of a suspicious looking person standing on the bank, staring motionless at the dock with a horrified look in her eyes. These whispers finally reached Elena and Sam. They closely peered at the person from a distance and soon realised it was poor Anna, still clutching her black handbag, her face pale and lifeless. The intense look of sheer terror shocked Elena and Sam to the core. They quickly ran towards her.

'Anna, is that you? What's happened? Anna, please say something,' Elena shouted in disbelief. All Anna could do was just stare at the ferry as people turned towards them. Elena held on to her sister-in-law's shoulder and shook violently to get her out of this state. Anna dropped the bag, but no one took a look inside.

'Anna, tell me, what's happened to the ferry?' Sam screamed.

Anna looked in the direction of his voice and instead of staring at the ferry, she now watched him for the longest time before she said, 'what are you doing here? I … I … punished you.'

'What do you mean, punished me? Anna what are you talking about? You're not making any sense,' Sam asked, stunned with what he heard.

'I killed you on the ferry, or at least I thought I did,' a mad Anna said.

'What? You were going to kill Sam? But then who did you murder on the ferry? Anna, speak to me!' Elena frantically yelled, and then the penny dropped. 'Oh no, for Heaven's sake… you killed Peter! You did, didn't you?' Elena felt sick to the stomach with what Anna had done. Her head began to spin; she felt dizzy and was about to faint, but Sam quickly broke Elena's fall.

After a while, Elena recovered from her faint. 'Oh, dear Lord, Anna… I can't believe it, why? Why did you do that?' she hollered, and promptly burst into a loud cry of unbearable pain.

¶

A petrified Anna began to slowly come out of shock as she was forced to listen to the tortured cries of Elena. Somewhere in her tangled and furious mind, she also started hearing other sounds of reality, like the voice of her son.

'Is that real or just my imagination?' she managed to whisper, referring to Adrian calling out to them.

'Oh Anna, for Heaven sake, what have you done?' a devastated Elena screamed at her again.

'Peter's on the ferry and you Sam are here. No, no, it can't be. Sam, please go and save my Peter. He might still be alive, please. Who did this? Tell me?'

'It was you Anna, you created this tragedy and it was you who killed your own husband,' Elena blurted out, not being able to control her words any longer.

'I hear Adrian. He's calling to us. He is there,' Anna cried, pointing downstream. 'Oh Lord, he must be somewhere near the waterfall!' Anna lamented and begged for mercy. 'Elena, Sam, my Adrian told me he wants to be a big king at the top of the world, where he would wait for his father to come to him. Oh, my Lord, my son is in very real danger! Please, save him! Let there not be another worthless death because of me,' she screamed her head off, quickly bent to pick up her handbag and ran towards the waiting carriage with Sam and Elena hot on her heels, following closely behind.

CHAPTER 14

With Peter still onboard, the ferry floated uncontrollably, turning and racing downstream at a fast rate of knots, towards the waterfall where Adrian waited for his father.

'Everyone get in. Quick!' Sam ordered. They jumped on the carriage and reached there as fast as they could. In fury, shock, and anger, Elena couldn't stop crying and cursing Anna for the situation now unfolding.

'You killed my brother. You're nothing but a murderer, Anna,' she kept repeating.

Anna, on the other hand, was in no condition to pay attention to anything. The one and only thing on her mind at this moment was Adrian's safety. She could feel it was already too late, where the boat might hit her son within minutes and he would die too. 'Go faster, Sam! Faster. Please save Adrian from a horrible death, like what his father just suffered.'

'Why did I do it? Peter, are you still alive, can you hear me? Please wake up and save our son. It's not too late,' she begged her dead husband, and started to feel paralysed with fear. Anna couldn't feel her legs, her hands were getting cold, her vision blurred, and her voice became slurred. She was completely broken from the inside, finding no ray of hope whatsoever.

Elena and Sam drove crazily towards the waterfall, while Anna sat motionless on the coach behind Sam, spurring him on. 'Hurry, my son's waiting on that God forsaken rock he's always talking about, for his father to come.' These words left her mouth so faint that she could hardly hear them herself.

¶

From a short distance, Sam saw the waterfall. Standing on top, was a happy and unaware Adrian, still calling out to his father.

'There he is!' Sam shouted, pointing towards Anna's son.

In the meantime, the ferry was hurtling along, unstoppable, towards the same spot.

'Adrian, we are here! We will come and get you,' Sam shouted.

This is when Adrian noticed quite a crowd of people gathered around him and enjoyed waving at his adoring subjects. 'Dad, look at me. I am the big king in my invisible glass house. Dad, can you hear me? This is a beautiful place to be. Come to me, I love you, Dad.'

The galloping horses had nearly reached where they needed to go, when Elena and Sam jumped out while the coach was still slowing down. They ran uphill towards Adrian through the shrubs, branches, grass, and rocks. Sam climbed on to the log that precariously hung over the river. They were so close to Adrian, yet so far, as both log and rock was surrounded by a tumultuous amount of stormy water.

¶

Anna, on the other hand, was still sitting in the coach like a lifeless stuffed animal. She kept whispering words which made no sense, to no one there.

Adrian, still unaware of the real situation, kept waving and yelling. 'Hey Dad, look! I'm the big King in my invisible palace!'

Vast amounts of water, churning and crashing on the rocks and upon itself made an unbearable and scary roar.

The horses standing near the river bank were becoming uneasy with the sound, and it looked as if they wanted to escape into the wild blue yonder.

Sam was still battling with his enemy, Time, and contemplated the quickest possible way to reach Anna's son. Adrian was on the rock, moving unsurely. Sam grabbed at whatever branches he could to help balance himself and crawled carefully along the log in order to reach Adrian with the utmost resolve. Sam's unshakable determination helped him to conquer his fears, and he finally managed to reach Adrian.

'Adrian, I'm here! Come to me, give me your hand. Quick now, give me your hand.'

'No, Mister Sam. Why must I come with you?' he questioned and before Sam could reply, Adrian continued. 'I'm the big king and this is my kingdom. I am strong, and I am safe.'

'Adrian, please listen and give me your hand now,' Sam

screamed in order to be heard, but the colossal uproar of falling water made communication difficult, both in terms of speech and listening.

'I'm waiting for my dad to come. Where is he? Why is he not coming?' Adrian asked.

'He is nearby,' Sam yelled. Suddenly, Adrian sensed that something was not quite right. With Sam's relentless persuasion, Adrian agreed to step off the rock.

Elena was seen to be anxiously watching nearby while crying and praying, hoping for the best possible outcome.

¶

Anna however, consumed by the clutches of insanity. Her blood was replaced with an inky black poison, and she wandered off in her mind without aim or ambition, having lost all purpose for living.

By now, the ferry was in very close proximity. Adrian pursued his earlier argument, which he felt he had failed to adequately convey to Sam. 'I am the big king. I will be back. This is my magic glass house. This is my kingdom. Mister Sam, will you come and visit me?'

'Yes, I absolutely will but for now, we must hurry. We have to meet your father. He's waiting for you, just around the corner, on the river bank,' Sam bellowed, in an undertone resembling great urgency.

'Sam, Sam! Hurry up, I see something approaching from upstream,' Elena wailed in sheer desperation.

Sam and Adrian cautiously anchored their foothold and stepped on to the dangerously slippery log.

The ferry was now within range of visible sight. Sam and Adrian quickened their pace. However, the water's resistance proved no match for the ferry's acquired momentum. Within the blink of an eye, the ferry collided with the rock. At this point, they had not quite reached the edge. With super human strength, Sam threw Adrian into Elena's open arms as he felt the full force of the ferry being pulverized into small fragments.

'Watch out, Sam!' Elena's warning was heard too late, and he was abruptly flung from the log and into the torrent of gushing water.

'Sam, Sam!' Elena let out a gut-wrenching scream. In her panic and fear, she watched his figure fade and disappear. 'Oh no, Sam… please don't leave me. Not you too, please no!'

Strong currents, accompanied by huge amounts of water, lifted the relatively light-weight ferry and other debris from their crash position, pushing it further towards the waterfall, where it simultaneously sank into its depths with the raging waters helping from above.

¶

Not too far away, another chapter of the Henderson drama is unfolding fast. Horrified and quite inconsolable as to what she had done, Anna slowly opened her handbag, pulled out the revolver, quickly pointed it at her chest and without a second thought, pulled the trigger.

For a few seconds, she stumbled, took her last breath, and died at the back of the coach where she had been sitting, waiting for Adrian, Sam, and Elena to return.

The sharp blast of the bullet frightened the horses and they immediately jumped and ran furiously ahead towards the tempestuous river with Anna as their submissive and uncomplaining passenger. All of a sudden, the coach hit a large rock and maintained inertia for a second before subsequently losing balance. The coach ploughed into the river, along with Anna, who was already dead. The horses were saved by some quick-thinking people standing nearby, who saw the whole thing happen.

Sadly, Elena saw this terrifying event take place as well. Thankfully, Adrian remained blissfully unaware of his mother's suicide. And within a matter of mere seconds, all identity, traces of evidence and existence of the shooting incidents were completely eradicated. As such, it would have been quite valid to have questioned whether Peter and Anna had ever lived at all.

'Oh no, no! Please God, no!' she yelped in huge shock and distress. Even though she could no longer see Anna, Elena decided to venture into the unforgiving depths of the Plym River to try and save her.

Adrian witnessed his aunt's frantic behaviour and, without understanding all the facts, he tried desperately to stop her. So, he forcefully grabbed her dress and asked to be hugged. Upon his desperate request, Elena took him into his arms and began to cry openly.

'No, no, Aunty Elena, please don't. I love you, please don't die. Please don't leave me alone,' Adrian appealed, kissed her on the hand and brought it close to his face. 'Please, don't leave me.'

Adrian began to sob, observing the great pain and sorrow within her eyes.

'Oh, dear child,' Elena struggled to pronounce these few simple words, as she felt helpless and hopelessly alone. She then knelt on the ground with tilted head towards the sky, and screamed, 'Oh dear God, why have you forsaken me? I've lost my brother, my sister-in-law, and Sam, who was my one and only true love. Lord, tell me now, what's the point in living anymore?' And then she wept.

Within that moment of golden silence, God answered her desperate call for help. 'Elena, a baby will someday grow within you. She will need your help. If you need a purpose, be sure to live, so you may give her life and love her forever more.'

After receiving this most unexpected message, this profound experience gave her new vision and hope.

Forlorn, Adrian continued sobbing. 'My dad didn't come to see me at my magic glass house. Why, tell me why?'

Elena felt awful as a result of all these painful events, which struck her hard.

'I'm … I'm not feeling so well,' she whispered inaudibly.

Because Adrian had his back to her, he did not see Elena fall to the ground, blacked out. It wasn't until he turned around again that he saw his aunty lying on the rough terrain.

'Aunty Elena, please aunty, you can't sleep now. Wake up, Aunty Elena,' he encouraged. Even a young child could tell something was badly wrong.

A few people standing close by saw what had just transpired, and quickly rushed to help both Elena and Adrian. 'What's happened, is everything alright, can we help?' they asked.

'Look there, the ferry has sunk into the deep waterfall. Why, tell me why? When will my dad come to me?'

Everyone was stunned, and no one knew what to say to make the poor child understand. Instead, they changed their focus towards helping Elena. 'Quickly, let's get her to the hospital.'

A small crowd gathered together, lifted Elena and put her and Adrian into someone else's waiting coach, and without wasting any further time, travelled fast towards the town. Adrian was still trapped in his own world thinking. Why did his dad not come to see him in the magical house upon the rock?

¶

Later in the hospital, Elena lay in bed, slipping in and out of consciousness. She was however, not aware that she was calling out for Sam, Adrian, Peter, and Anna. The doctor wondered about who all these people were.

After a while, she became fully alert and returned to the harsh reality of life. 'Are they here? Will they come?' she mentioned, still in shock.

'Miss Henderson, please relax,' the doctor suggested quietly and asked her about the names she spoke of before.

'Oh doctor, those people are sadly all dead, except for little Adrian.' She went back into stress mode and started crying.

'Oh, I'm so sorry, Miss Henderson,' the doctor gently mentioned. 'Please accept my deepest sympathy for the death of your brothers, Sam and Peter, as well as your sister, Anna.'

So, engulfed in her own grief, she didn't even notice the jumbled-up relationships mentioned by the doctor.

'Oh Lord, what am I supposed to do now? What will happen next?' she complained, with palms covering her face in despair.

'Miss Henderson, life continues to move forward and so will you,' he tried to redirect her mind in a more positive way.

'Oh no, no… Sam rescued Adrian from the waterfall and in so doing, he sadly lost his own life. Why is this happening to me?' she asked, weeping uncontrollably.

'Miss Henderson, your brother took extraordinary steps to put his life at risk to save your younger sibling.' The doctor remained unaware of who was who, still trying desperately to offer her some comforting words.

'You've got it all wrong, doctor. Sam was not my brother. He was the man I loved, and met him while he was on vacation here. He was due to return home tomorrow and now he will never finish his study.'

The doctor accepted her words and apologised for the mix up, then requested for Elena to take the prescribed medication and hastily left the room, unable to cope with weeping females.

CHAPTER 15

What really did happen to Sam?

When the ferry hit the log with him standing on it, the log swung with full force and became stuck in between two smaller rocks. With its full impact, he rolled down to the other side of the river bank and hurt himself. It was a miracle, but he was still alive. He lay on the ground, comatose.

When he regained consciousness a few hours later, he stood, looked around, and tried to figure out what had happened? All around him, water tumbled without mercy. He found himself in a place where no one could come to his aid.

'Elena, Adrian! Where are you?' he kept calling out to them. 'Oh Lord, please tell me they are still alive?' He then turned his attention towards both Peter and Anna, and questioned why this tragedy came about? He now wanted only one thing: to get out of this hell hole of a place, so he could go and check on Elena and Adrian. In excruciating, physical pain, he pulled himself together and decided to make a move but where to. And how?

I know, I'll go upstream along the river and then continue on my way into town. Yes, that's the only way to rescue myself from these unknown surroundings.

Somewhat partially wounded, along with being thoroughly soaked and cold, Sam was determined to follow his plan, and started limping upstream. Completely exhausted, he was covering this torturous track, by walking at a snail's pace; stopping occasionally to catch his breath. Some thirty minutes passed by, when he suddenly heard an approaching coach. Perhaps he could catch a lift.

'Hey, are you alright there, mister? I see you're limping badly,' the man in the coach asked Sam with some concern.

In great agony, he looked pleadingly at the rider and gasped for air, but could not say anything,

The caring stranger hurriedly jumped from the coach and joined him at ground level. 'Oh, my boy, you're soaking wet and exhausted. How come? What's wrong? What's happened?' the man asked with compassion.

Sam was still unable to speak.

'Hey boy, where are you headed?' the farmer asked, trying to gather at least some clue about the situation this poor man has found himself in.

'To town please, I'm heading towards home,' Sam was able to say, at last, with great difficulty.

'Oh, my boy, you puzzle me. What dreadful thing has befallen you?' Sam's saviour questioned, attempting to dredge up some more useful information.

'Waterfall,' Sam replied and had to sit on a nearby rock.

'Oh, of course,' the farmer replied but still wondered about what he meant. 'I tell you, I heard a lot of loud commotion and echoing going on with a big bang in the vicinity of the waterfall but I thought my old ears were getting a bit rusty and were hearing things that were not there. You know what I mean?' he said, as he looked at this miserable wet wretch sitting before him. 'Well my boy, I will give you a lift into town, as I'm heading there myself.'

'Thank you, mister. I would greatly appreciate it,' Sam sincerely said.

The kind farming man helped Sam climb onto his coach. Once securely on board, he whipped the horses and kept talking, in order to make polite conversation. 'My boy, don't tell me you tried to swim in that big waterfall but- by the look of you, I see that you did. You must be raving crazy.'

Sam did not try to reply and ground his teeth instead.

'My boy, because you remain silent, I must be correct? Anyway, I imagine somebody climbed to that big rock at the top and hollered their head off. I reckon only a dumb person could do that. A strong river current can be a very tricky business to play with, which could easily cost a person's life in one easy click of a finger. It can happen real fast and I can tell you this from personal experience. I nearly lost my life here too, when crossing the waterfall and I slipped on some mossy wet rocks. Luckily, I grabbed hold of an overhanging shrub in order to stop myself from falling into the water completely and thankfully, I was able to walk away, largely unhurt. And as you can see, I'm still alive. But my boy, this story does not have a happy ending. My beloved and treasured wife accidentally drowned not far from where the ferry is normally moored,' he said, which made him cry. With great sorrow, wiped away his tears.

'I'm so sorry for your unexpected loss. It must have been terrible for you,' Sam said.

'Well, son, that's life but you, my boy, promise me you'll be happy and not sad- like me. But I must also warn you, don't ever think of trying again to swim or climb on that God-awful wet stuff. What's your name, by the way?'

'Adrian,' Sam quietly mentioned, heavy in thought and mental exhaustion.

'Adrian's a mighty fine name. My name is Thomas, but people call me Tom for short,' he said, as he introduced himself. The farmer abruptly hit his horses with great strength, which caused the coach to move more violently over the rough ground.

'Oh no, please stop! Not so fast,' Sam screamed in agony.

'I'm sorry. I didn't think, but we can adopt a more leisurely pace, if this is what will make you feel more physically comfortable,' he said and pulled on the harness belts, so the horses obeyed the instruction from their master to go slower.

Sam glanced at the farmer, thinking of him as a kind man. To confirm Sam's evaluation of his good character, Tom opened a brown paper bag and offered him a piece of bread.

'Adrian, come on, take it. That's all I have to offer. It tastes a whole lot better than those you can buy in the shop. I cooked it myself. All you have to do is just mix up some corn flour, yeast, and water. Then bake in a bed of hot coals and there you have it- one tasty loaf of homemade bread.'

Sam gratefully took and ate it without hesitation. He

also noticed Tom called him Adrian, but did not bother to correct him.

'Tell me, boy, what do you do for a living, besides swimming?' Tom asked, as he was genuinely interested in knowing about who Sam was.

'I am an agronomist, Tom. I've been here on holiday for the past five weeks, staying with my parents, helping them around the house and in the fields. I am due to leave tomorrow, for my own home in London, so I may resume my course of study.'

'Oh well, this explains everything. I know such people love all that wet stuff in order to grow better crops that can, on a regular basis, bear appetising fruit and veggies. In fact, I would straight away employ you in my own field, because I desperately need someone like you as well but right now, you are sick, and you need a doctor. So, have no fear and don't worry about anything, my boy. I'll make sure I take you to the best one in town. His name is Doctor Jack, a truly marvellous man, who has the Midas touch. He cured me well and truly. I once went to him with a big pop-up ugly ulcer on my body, which was huge like a chook egg. And guess what happened? He made some fine cuts to the ulcer and squeezed hard. A great deal of pus, like volcano lava, splashed all over him! As you can imagine, I yelped with excruciating pain, but the good doctor stood there and burst out laughing at my hair-raising predicament. As he, in all his life as a doctor, had never seen so much pus erupt from one ordinary ulcer. I thanked him and freely put money in his pocket. He asked why? I said it was to pay for the dry cleaning of his overcoat. I figured, fair is only fair.'

As they got closer to their destination, Tom changed the subject and continued. 'Well. Adrian! It won't be long now, as we have nearly reached the hospital.'

Sam listened to him speak with not much concentration. 'Oh Anna, how on earth could you do something like that?' he softly said.

Tom heard his words though. 'Anna, who is she, my boy, and what has she done to you?' Tom asked, with piqued curiosity.

'It was she who killed the ferry man, Peter Henderson, her own husband!' Sam confessed.

'My boy, what do you mean? I can't believe it!' Tom was shocked to hear such an absurd story. He promptly stopped the coach and turned towards Sam, to look at him, face to face and man to man. 'Adrian my boy, is that really ridgy didge true? No, it couldn't possibly be her. Are you absolutely certain?' he asked totally aghast and horrified.

All Sam could do was nod in reply to Tom's last question.

'It must be a mistake. And if it's not, she must not have been of sound mind. I know Anna well. She is a faithful woman who loved her husband dearly.'

'I'm sorry, Tom. It was Anna and it's no mistake, for that I am certain,' Sam confirmed.

'I still can't believe it. Peter's actually dead, killed by his wife's hand. Please, with your permission, I'd like to go and see the site where this hideous crime has taken place. So, I may believe the words you spoke of are true,' the farmer proposed.

⁊

Sam agreed, as they headed off in the direction where the ferry had once been moored. People were still milling about, thinking, wondering, and speaking about this recent calamity in their small community.

Once again standing on his own two feet, Tom glanced at the place where the ferry used to be.

'But I don't see anything here. What's happened to the whereabouts of Anna and the ferry? Did she take the ferry to Heaven too?' Tom asked, quite confused and distraught. Being a God-fearing and church-going citizen, he automatically made the sign of the cross. Sam however, was eventually able to convince Tom that this was the truth and that Anna did indeed kill Peter.

'My boy, let's get you to the doctor now, post haste.' Without a second glance back, they returned to the waiting carriage and headed off towards the hospital.

⁊

'Here we are,' Tom mentioned as they approached the hospital grounds. 'Listen, Jack's an exceptional doctor. You'll be alright with him and he'll make you better in no time. You're also lucky he will treat you for those minor injuries that you have. But he won't if you should be suffering from any big, volcano erupting ulcers,' Tom laughingly said.

'Thank you, Tom, for giving me a lift. I don't believe I would have made it this far without your help.'

'Just promise you won't do anything so stupid as to go swimming in the waterfall again.'

Sam gave Tom his word, turned and began to limp towards the entrance, where he knew he would receive expert care.

Acknowledging Adrian would be okay from here on in, the farmer knew this was his cue to continue his own way forward.

§

Sam patiently sat in the corridor while waiting for someone to come and help him. Finally, without really giving him a second glance, the sister-in-charge who was stationed in the office opposite to where he was sitting, opened the window wide, to speak with him.

'Can I help you, please?' she asked politely.

'Can I kindly see Doctor Jack, please?' he requested.

'What's your name, sir? And why do you wish to see the doctor?' she replied in a professional and business-like tone.

'My name is Sam Prescot, and I'm desperate to see him about my recent injuries, obtained only a few hours ago.'

This time, she took a proper look at him. Seeing with her own eyes and without delay, she called the doctor to join them. He quickly came and looked at a cold, wet, and sorry Sam. In an instant and without doing any tests, he realised this man was indeed in some pain.

'Please, follow me, sir,' the doctor mentioned and immediately took him to the consulting room.

¶

'So, Mister Prescot, I am here to help you,' he mentioned, while shaking his head in frustration. 'I'm not particularly interested in how, why, and where you've been swimming or bathing, but it seems to me you've been on some wild adventure, which brings you here to be cured of your injuries.'

Sam tried to correct the doctor's wrong impression of the circumstances, but found it difficult to speak, so let the matter go.

The doctor proceeded with the initial examination. After the testing was finished, he said, 'you are a bit of an unusual case sir. You've got a bruised shoulder, your elbow is swollen, your legs are shaking, and you have difficulty in breathing. And I would not be doing my job properly if I did not suggest you stay overnight. To let your body rest and heal to some degree, which will allow you to be discharged from hospital tomorrow.'

'Oh no, I can't do that. I have my parents to think about and look after. I should be with them. They'll be worried about me.'

Sam clearly did not like the idea of staying overnight, but on the doctor's advice, he was given no option but to agree. Doctor Jack prescribed some medication for him and began talking about the recent ferry accident, still fresh in everyone's mind.

'Mister Prescot, did you hear about this most tragic event with the ferry that has struck this tranquil town real bad?

Where the traditional Henderson ferry ownership has come to an abrupt end? But I'm most happy to report that in this particular tragedy, one miracle person did survive and is well on their way to making a full and speedy recovery,' he claimed, while shaking his head in disbelief.

'Doctor, pray tell, who is this miracle person you speak of?' Sam hurriedly asked.

'I've just finished treating this patient and like you, they'll be discharged tomorrow as well,' mentioned the doctor. This is when the nurse entered the room and no more could be said about that.

'Please nurse, can you take Mr Prescot to his room,' he instructed and obediently, she did as she was told, and added to Sam, 'I'll see you in the morning.'

¶

Later that night, while the doctor was writing his daily report, he began to put the pieces of the jigsaw puzzle together, remembering the information given by both patients during the day.

Hmm, it is a most interesting situation indeed, with no real clear answers yet. Take Sam Prescot for example. The doctor remembered Elena correcting him earlier when she said Sam was not her brother. That he was in fact, the man she loved so much. She also mentioned Sam tried to rescue Adrian at the big waterfall, which is when Sam lost his life by drowning, as a result of the ferry crashing at full speed into the log he was standing on. *Now I discover for myself that Sam is very much alive, well, and sleeping peacefully in the room next door. Oh well, tomorrow is another day in which I can clear up this mystery.* And believed that all Sam needed was a good night's rest, as did he. Upon thinking this, the doctor switched off the office light and went home, leaving the hospital to be run by the capable hands of the night nurse.

¶

On the very next day, the first thing Doctor Jack did was to check the patient records, to see who were to be discharged. He requested for Nurse Morgan to prepare only two reports: one for Elena Henderson and the other for Sam Prescot.

He then went to Elena's room and reminded her she was going home. Before leaving on his normal morning rounds, the doctor casually mentioned, in a subtle kind of way, about the man from the waterfall.

'Yesterday, some hours after you came in, Miss Elena, I had an interesting consultation with a young male patient, who, when he arrived, was soaking wet and shivering. He told me he came from the waterfall, which is where he obtained his injuries and which I have now treated successfully.'

'A man you said… And may I ask, what's his name?' she asked somewhat impatiently.

The doctor half evaded her question by saying, 'well, my dear, all I can say is that he's being sent home today as well. So,

I suggest you better get yourself ready and come down as soon as you can to the patient waiting room. And please, bring this discharge letter with you when you come.'

'Yes, I will, doctor. Thank you,' she said, feeling much happier than yesterday, knowing that she would soon be returning to the security of her own home. That is when the nurse entered.

'Nurse Morgan, can you please kindly take this lady to the patient waiting room when she's ready?' Doctor Jack requested.

'Yes, most certainly, doctor,' the nurse replied, and after helping Elena to get ready for her departure, she escorted her to her final destination in the hospital environment.

The doctor then casually paid a visit to Sam and looked at him with some suspicion. 'Mister Prescot, today I shall let you go. So please, get yourself organised and bring this discharge letter to the patient waiting room as quickly as you can.'

Ten minutes later, the doctor held out his hand to Elena. 'Ah, I see you are ready to leave us now, Miss Henderson. Please take care of yourself and we hope not to see you back here again too soon.'

'Thank you again, Doctor Jack, for everything you've done for me. I am most grateful for your help and advice,' she said, and shook his hand before walking out the nearby door.

At the same time as Elena was halfway out the exit door, Sam entered the waiting room and saw a woman leaving. Seeingher briefly from behind, she felt somewhat familiar to him and sensed he knew her.

'Doctor, who was the woman who just left?' he hastily asked. 'I'm only saying that, because I think I know her.'

'Oh, that was my patient, Miss Henderson. She was bought in yesterday by some strangers who stopped to help her where the tragic accident occurred. Why, do you know her?' he asked.

'Who did you say? Henderson! Oh, my Lord, it is her! Elena, Elena!' Sam shouted in disbelief and ran out the door at lightning speed. 'Elena, Elena!' he called out loudly, once again.

She heard her name, recognised his voice, swung around, and couldn't believe her eyes.

'Sam! Sam is it really you?' she yelled back and rushed to meet him halfway, where they threw themselves into each other's arms. He lifted her up and kissed her eagerly. Elena returned his kiss with equal passion and abandonment.

'Oh, my darling, I still can't believe my eyes. Oh, Sam, I was convinced that you died trying to save Adrian, but here you are, very much alive and kicking. Praise the Lord. I thought I had lost you forever.' She couldn't stop crying great tears of happiness and joy.

'Elena, my darling, I love you so much. I didn't think I would ever see you again. Thank God you are here with me now.' He too was crying. They firmly hugged each other, and it was in such a state, they stayed for a long time.

Meanwhile, Doctor Jack stood in the doorway to the hospital, looking at the happy couple embrace, smiled and shook his head in amazement. The mystery he was confronted with the day before was resolved in this extraordinary drama of two young people in love. He wished them only the best of British luck for their future and that they may have a prosperous life together. The doctor hoped that if he was lucky, he may get an invitation to their wedding in the near future.

In his excitement, Doctor Jack turned too quickly and as an unfortunate consequence, hit his head, and rubbed it better before walking inside to continue his day of healing the sick and injured.

Chapter 16

Elena later adopted Adrian to be as her own son, to look after, care and support as his own parents would have wanted her to do. For a little child, it was extremely hard to understand why his mum and dad left him so abruptly and were never coming back home. He kept on asking Elena some really serious questions as to why he could never see them again, of which she had no answer.

'Where is Daddy? Where is my mum? Why did my dad not come and see me when I was in my magic glass house, on top of the world?' These questions would haunt him for a long time. Simply because no bodies were ever retrieved. In his young eyes, they were not necessarily dead, just missing.

Later, after many years had passed by, Adrian did grow up to be an intelligent young man. This is when he began to understand and accept the harsh reality that his parents can't be with him in a physical sense, and how they were now watching over him from Heaven above.

In this brand-new environment, Elena and Adrian became very close and lived together with a great deal of mutual respect, harmony, humour, and love for each other.

Sam Prescot did return to the university and finished

his Degree in Agronomy. Once accomplished, he returned to Plymouth to live with Elena as man and wife, along with Adrian, their adopted son. Three years into their marriage and as God promised in an earlier premonition, Elena gave birth to a healthy baby girl, called Adriana. They knew that Anna in particular would have loved that name.

The End